PURE HOLLYWOOD

PURE HOLLYWOOD

Christine Schutt

SHEFFIELD – LONDON – NEW HAVEN

First published in the United Kingdom in 2018 by And Other Stories
Sheffield – London – New Haven
www.andotherstories.org

First published in the US in 2018 by Grove Atlantic.

9 8 7 6 5 4 3 2 1

This book is a work of fiction. Any resemblance to actual persons, living or dead, events or places is entirely coincidental.

ISBN: 978-1-911508-24-3
eBook ISBN: 978-1911508-25-0

Proofreader: Sarah Terry; Typesetter: Tetragon, London; Typefaces: Linotype Neue Swift and Verlag; Cover Design: Abby Weintraub; Cover Photograph: Hamish Robertson. Printed and bound by the CPI Group (UK) Ltd, Croydon, CRO 4YY.

A catalogue record for this book is available from the British Library.

This book was supported using public funding by Arts Council England.

To David

CONTENTS

How disappointing it was to wake intact and far away from the matchstick aftermath of the extinguished fires, thready smoke rising from piles that had been homes, the famous modern house not among them.

"Mimi?" he asked quietly, driving up a slight incline and into a space still hers, everything, all of it: a modern house shaped like slung plates, no corners, different heights. "What do they think this place is worth?" he asked, still whispering so as not to disturb – what? There was only the house.

"What's it worth? It's like living in a great fucking painting is what it is. The place is priceless." The house was not that much cooler than the car, and Mimi went through it and opened windows and the sliding door to the terrace. "I know I'm letting in hot air," she said, "but I hate things shut." She moved off to the kitchen and offered Stetson a drink.

"What are you doing?" he asked as he found and filled two glasses with ice.

"I'm taking off my clothes," she said. "They smell of smoke. I should go ahead and burn them." Off came her shell and the wavy pants that shivered down the chair rail as fast as she threw them. Underneath she wore what looked like string. There wasn't much to her.

"Fuck," Stetson said. His shirt was off, his pants, his shoes. He sniffed his arm. "My arm stinks." He put his arm up to his sister's nose. "What is that?"

"Pickles?" she offered. "What did you have for lunch?"

He sniffed his other arm. "Nothing."

All the pleasure to be had in looking at Stetson but Mimi had married Arnold Fine, ugly as an anvil, Arnie, and driven her brother away. Less than a month ago her husband stepped into the pool and died. Age sixty-nine, heart attack – happened fast and what happened after came on faster: the ambulance, the body bag, the funeral home, the furnace. He was ashes in a matter of minutes.

Mimi poured vodka into her glass. "Tonic," she pointed to the counter, "and there's Perrier."

Tap was okay with Stetson but did she have any food?

"How can you be hungry! Smell your arm," she said.

Wearing pointy mules, Mimi walked onto the terrace to a Hockney scene, only not so blue, more green. The lounge chairs were rightly low and wide, hewn from wood that would outlast them, but the pool? Mimi said, "The pool's a swampy squiggle, I'm afraid, decorative. What do you think it's worth?" she asked and watched him assess the place. "This is like old times," Mimi said, and walked into the water to her waist.

"You're tempting me," he said. "How do you insure a priceless place?"

"You don't." For a time she stared at the house, then walked out of the pool and took up her glass and banged the cubes against her teeth, chewed ice.

She adjusted her strings, distracted by leaves wooden in the wind. If only the wind weren't so hot.

"Is there someone here?" Stetson asked.

"The gardener?" A gardener seemed to have come with the house, a man not so new as ignored. The gardener had a leaf blower. The plants weren't a problem but the grotesque tree shed. Brown leaves, long as shoes, got shuffled around the walkways until the nameless gardener came to blow them out of sight. They disappeared, just as the gardener disappeared, week to week. Sometimes Mimi heard the hacking cough of his truck; sometimes, his blower. Today she had heard nothing; there was nothing much to blow away; nothing dead in the pool, but the slack hose jumped, distended, and withdrew around the house, followed by the sound of water. It had to be the gardener.

Mimi went to see and, yes, it was the gardener misting the front of the house. He had nodded at her. What was wrong with him? Didn't he read the papers? Someone — not Mimi, not today — would have to tell him there was no more work here. She walked back to Stetson, enjoying the katack-katack of her shoes against the stone terrace, a sound both slutty and indulgent, right out of the movies, but wasn't Mimi right out of the movies? She was pretty enough – everyone said.

"Does this really feel like home to you?" he asked.

"Yes," she said and she adjusted the chair to lie flat, eyes closed, given over to the liquidy heat lapping her pale body.

"We weren't married long enough for anyone to believe I loved Arnie," she said, "but I did. He made me laugh. Honestly. Aren't you hot?" she sat up, wiped her eyes, and walked into the pool. "Come in with me. The water's cold, but you get used to it."

If his sister was thin, he was thin, too, jailbird-sickly with his arms held up as he waded in, testing. The pool was not very deep, which might explain the slightly yellow color of the water, and the sky, too, was a creepy kind of yellow, a spreading dread.

"Do you think . . ." she began and didn't finish. She said, "The gardener's hosing down the house."

"When's the last time this pool was cleaned?" Stetson treaded water and looked around him. "Just the color," he said, which, along with slimy tiles, was sickening, and he did his swimming, such as it was, in the middle. He dived under; he made a few strokes down and back. Only the tiles along the ledge of the pool seemed unclean, and he avoided the ledge until the last minute when he lifted himself out.

"Hey," she said, "where're you going?"

"Inside."

In the kitchen, he refilled his glass and drank enough to fill it again before he set it on the counter. His medicine made him thirsty. Mimi came up from behind him and he flinched at her touch.

Water splattered against the windows – the gardener was close.

"You don't get it."

"I do," she said, "you're sober and I'm not."

He said, "That's right," then he took up his glass and walked down the hall into the bathroom, where a clunking noise signaled his intention to shower. From the looks of the soap – discolored, cracked – no one had used the downstairs shower for some time. Tepid reddish water pooled at his corpsey feet and the clunk of the pipes when he turned off the water echoed, sounding spooky. He couldn't do much with a hand towel, and his long hair dripped onto his collar and down the back of his white shirt. At least he felt cool; at least dressing and the hotter prospects of the hours to come didn't dismay him. But his sister, just getting past her was hard. Mimi stood, almost as he'd left her, in the kitchen, listening to nothing he could hear, but her expression suggested the sound grated.

"What is it?"

"You don't hear that? Not the pipes. There it is again."

All he heard was the high-pitched present.

"Stay," she said.

"I can't," he said and said again to himself as he backed onto a steep road that wound through the dry brush down the hillside, past other drives and tucked-away houses. The houses he could see were messy blots on other hills, expensive blots. Stetson didn't have much money but whose fault was that? He knew that's what his sponsor would say: Why not whine home to Daddy and ask? Some sponsor.

The late afternoon sky he saw was the same Mimi saw leached of all its color. Mimi, with her eyes stung by the smoke or crying or both, drew the draperies and turned on a downstairs light, a small flame in the gloom of the mostly bare and sunken living room. The Eames chair – her husband's – startled her: where had it been that she had not seen it? Then her lawyer, making good on his word, called, and she learned what she already knew: nothing was hers.

Briefly sober, she called Stetson's cell to say she wasn't going to drink anymore and she wished he would come back. She didn't like to be alone in the house. "I want to get better. I want to get over this. I wish you'd pick up," she said, then blipped off, hurt to think he hadn't even answered a call with her name. She fixed herself more of the same and lowered the blinds in the kitchen and in the dining room to spy on the gardener as he moved around the house. His expression was hard to make out, but she watched him wrestle the hose into a terra-cotta pot; the hose must have weighed more than he did, poor man. When she thought he might come to the front door, Mimi took off her mules and crept through the house, up the floating staircase to what she had made into her bedroom, where she hid between the bed and the wall. She waited, she waited for a long time, which was perhaps what he did, the gardener, in his garden colors. He stood outside the door in good faith of payment but for what? Hosing down the house against fires, mounting staghorn ferns? What had he done today, this gardener, and why was it she knew him only as shadowy and poor? His stunted children rest their chins on the kitchen table. Sticky fly strips hang near the sink and back door. His wife's scorched hair is in the rice and on his tongue; now the rice tastes dirty. Look elsewhere – forget the shapeless face of his fat son, there is his favorite there, his daughter, over there near the fly strips shaking cinnamon on everything she eats. "Even beans?" he asks her.

The gardener, where was he now? The gardener's truck was gone – the gardener was gone, left without being paid: now how will he feed those children?

* * *

Driving east into the sensation of a rising sun, driving into mountains made no more attractive than dung by that same sun not seen, not seen – Stetson was driving without any music, and Jesus – it hurt to look at it, the desert house as he remembered it: a rusted box on stilts and the garden, made of white crushed rock and cacti, too forbidding to play near although their mother sat among the stolid barrelheads, plinking the pink spines in her cloud of absence. She liked to smoke and watch the sun drop behind the mountains on the other side of which were the Pacific and their father. Mother said their father was watching the same sky, but how did she know this?

"I do."

When she said, "I do," she would pout in the way she used to as an actress and for a moment she was Sabine Agard again and not their mother.

Why weren't they in school? Their mother said they could make up the weeks missed in summer at home in LA. Their mother made a face Sabine Agard made in movies: shifty. She turned away. On the baked stone she sat, barrel-like and spined in fishhook spines too fine to see, yet they knew enough not to brush against their mother. They sat quietly and waited out the sky until it dulled.

Mimi's job was to fry eggs for a breakfast-dinner; Stetson's to put out plates. They made a lot of noise; it felt good. Turned on the radio and the Mexican guys in sombreros sang "Las Mañanitas."

Great cracks from the bacon Mimi poked made them jump and roused their mother, who sniffed her way in but looked through them. The bacon buckled and the yolks broke.

"Careful," Mother said but too late. Grease prickled Mimi's arms and she yelped. No long good night tonight, they knew. No books, no songs, no prayers, no promises; no stories about when, When you were born . . . When you were two . . . Was there ever a time before them – really?

Yes. Since they had moved to the desert Mother thought most about what happened before with people they didn't remember or hadn't known.

Stetson shunned the eggs and stuck wadded fat from the bacon up his nose.

"That's disgusting!" Mimi cried.

But their mother was already gone.

Best not think about how she did it, how half in and out of the bed she was, pills, goblets – gobbets, blood? Even then he was thinking of soldiers and dragons and fortifications.

You didn't see anything. I didn't either.

Mimi told the helpline their mother wasn't waking up but that their mother was alive.

How did Mimi know that?

I didn't. I was afraid. I got you out of the house. Do you remember? We sat in the cactus garden. The sun wasn't over the mountains and the desert was cool. After a while an ambulance came. He could only pretend to remember. Everything about his mother's suicide came from newspapers and magazines.

Stetson was nine years old at the time; Mimi was eleven. Someone drove them to a little airport, put them on a little plane. They knew they were going to their father because his name was repeated, Jack Deminthe, Mr. Deminthe, said in tones that made him out to be an important man working from afar.

Jack Deminthe, at seventy, masseused and smooth as a skinned almond, orderly and fit, no swollen or discolored parts about him but he attended to them, got himself fixed, saw the right doctor, bought a better, more expensive chair or piece of equipment to pedal. He was pedaling now at home alone and watching while on the TV fires unevenly advanced again in the Malibu Hills. He was safe but his daughter wasn't, was she? Jack had warned Mimi: comedians don't retire; they just get more depressed. Arnie Fine, once a funnyman, had died of a curdled heart. How many times had Jack told her: Arnie Fine will not make you laugh.

But she had insisted he did. Arnie may have made others cry, but not her. Mimi had said he was funny to her. "What's odd is that a comedian would marry someone like me with no sense of humor," and then in a sly voice, "Must be something else about me," which even to remember made Jack uncomfortable.

Later in the morning, Jack Deminthe told his trainer about Arnie Fine, not mentioning his daughter Mimi.

The trainer had never heard of Arnie Fine. The trainer was from one of those places in Eastern Europe that Jack associated with mass graves in the woods and wet wool coats. "I don't know this man!" he shouted. Everything the trainer said came out loud, but to be fair, when Jack thought about it, as a Chechen, the poor bastard had probably survived by being loud.

For lunch Jack had a vegetarian concoction – kale, lemon, mint – an astringent drink that made his blood fizz. He drank water, several glasses of water, along with the kale juice. His lunch companion, his secretary, Jody, had the same.

"How does that make you feel?" Jack asked.

"Full?"

Whereto after lunch but Walmart for slippers. He needed new slippers. Jack had his driver take him to

Walmart and the two of them walked through the store until they found slippers. "Everyone in this country is fat," Jack said, and he made no effort to be discreet but repeated himself as he sensed approach, which happened from time to time, so that he said something repellent, something about the aisle and its width, the supersized quantities of crap. He considered a tub of mayonnaise.

Jack let his driver pay for the slippers but before he could take up the receipt, he heard the low utterance of his name and was ruffled by the flurry of two women passing. In the car Jack told his driver the next stop was Malibu. He wanted to see for himself: was the famous house still standing?

Yes, the house, a stacked appearance as of a backbone, he could just see it, the house named after its architect, Alessandro Piro, the Piro house was upright. Jack could see it as the car took the last turn, but was his daughter in it?

He should know but they had stopped speaking when Mimi told him she had married Arnie Fine.

At home again, in the room he called a study despite the toys in it – treadmill, golf clubs, small weights – Jack called Stetson.

"If you're so worried, Dad, why don't you call her?" For his part, Stetson was sorry for whatever legal tangle Mimi was in with Arnie Fine's children – children decades older than Mimi. "The man's dead. Call her for condolences at least."

"Oh, Mimi," Jack said when he called his daughter and listened for as long as he could to what she had done and what she had yet to do. The reading of the will? An auction? Jack Deminthe didn't understand any of it. "Mimi, whatever were you thinking?"

"Nothing I've done so far would suggest I'm very bright, Dad."

"The eyes should be just about here," Arnie said, and he pointed: two tiny frown crescents above his cheeks. If his cheeks were red, he would have looked like a sad elf, but Arnie's skin was a sallow yellow, dingy where he shaved, and he shaved poorly, so he looked like an ill-intentioned elf with black bristles and acne scars, fat creases serving as a neck. A face hard to touch much less kiss, and he knew it. He didn't care, had never cared, or maybe didn't care anymore, what was the difference? He was rich, he was funny. His face was funny. The bowling-ball shape of his head was classically funny. Also, the baldness helped. Was there ever a fat comedian with a lot of hair? Probably, but the ones that came to mind who looked like him, the Don Rickleses of the world, had withering hairlines. Fine was more of a bawdy comic – he wasn't unkind. He loved women and bemoaned his bad luck with them.

And his wife? He had always loved Ruthie no matter what anyone said, but celebrity and money had made him more attractive to women at sixty than at any other time in his life. Bimbos, starlets, yeah, sure, breasts solid as hams with anuses no bigger than his pinkie, but . . . fuck-all – a girl underage for fucking sure on a frigid night in Minnesota found at the back door with a spiral notebook and a crumby pen: it dried out just as he was signing. "This fucking cold," he said and saw her tears – from him or from the cold? "Ever been in a limousine?" he asked. "Want to take a ride and warm up with me? I've a driver," he said. "You can show me what to see." He was tired after that tour, bone-tired, deep-tired, something . . . Must have been around that time Mimi Deminthe found him. He wasn't exactly looking but Mimi Deminthe liked him. "Do you feel safe with me?" he asked. "Of course," she said, "You know who my father is, don't you?" So he took advantage of the moment and the money he had made, money enough to have a famous house and a fast car, and time on his hands to let a young woman, who loved to drive, drive anywhere. If he had reasons to suspect his heart was clogged, he overlooked them. Let her drive fast. Let her try her hand at whatever might make her happy.

* * *

Arnie Fine was gone and in his place stood his son Donald with look-alike cheeks buckshot from acne, a sad inheritance, but not so Mimi's. On good days she could see her mother's face in hers. (Today, with the lawyers and auctioneers at the Piro house, her face was entirely her own and crooked.) And Arnie's daughter? Mimi figured Patricia Fine for an updated Ruthie, the late great long-sufferer who had shoved Arnie Fine through the 1980s, made him famous if not sober. Ruth Gabel Fine, with her frizzy red hair, small eyes, mother to the lumpen twosome, had led Donald Fine to believe he was charming. Upon their meeting, he had put his heavy hands on Mimi's shoulders and looked at her approvingly, saying, "Now I get it." He said, "No wonder we never met before." He said, "How old are you?" and he winked to let her in on – what? At least Patricia Fine ignored her. Patricia Fine had come to the Piro house for a painting.

"The Diebenkorn, Patty? Really? Since when did you even notice it?"

"Don't call me *Patty*."

"I mean you've never expressed interest in Dad's art before. Do you even know what it's called? Okay," he said, but his sister kept her back to him unyielding.

"Patricia," he said, and then emphatically, "Patricia?"

In the Piro house and ever alert for cover, Mimi had a foot on the stair for the guest bedroom and the gully between the bed and the wall, the curtain, the window from which vantage she had spied on the gardener, the gardener she could not pay. He had waited at the door. The gardener, indistinguishable, blending against the shedding eucalyptus in its dead bowl of shaggy bark, she missed him and all the easy days she was married.

"Miss?"

"Deminthe," she said, "but I'm still the widow."

"Yes," he said, "I'm aware." This man with his hand on her arm, a man not family but employed, maybe an overseer, a caretaker, a lawyer, a guard, an auctioneer, gestured toward the herding warmth of the Fines – a pack of them, old cousins with old children, an ancient uncle with a menacing walker.

Mimi pointed up the stairs – her intent.

"It's a viewing," he said. "First floor only."

"But I'm not interested in anything," she said.

"No one's to go upstairs," he said.

"My room's upstairs." She said, "I'm not entirely moved out."

"I'm sorry, miss."

"I'm the wife," she said. "I'm the fucking widow."

"I'm sorry."

She veered away from Mr. Security and walked toward a corner, out of the way. What was it she had said to Stetson about the Piro house? Priceless? Last week it had seemed invulnerable in all the ways Arnie had said it was – none of the fires ever came close.

An important house, one of its kind, like great classic cars, Maserati, Ferrari, Mustang, it was a work of art, irreplaceable. Inside the important house was another matter. The tubular furniture – a lot of it unfriendly – was gone, but its absence hardly enlarged the downstairs spaces crowded with inheritors shoving in to see the art and counting up play money. Patricia Fine circled the Diebenkorn, flicked a notebook, looked elsewhere, looked out the sliding glass windows to the terrace and the pool where her father had died.

Mimi had found him, Arnie, facedown in the water; no chance for a funny last line – "This is no way to live."

Had Arnie known he had so little time left, he might have spent it differently. As it was, his wife was dead and he didn't particularly like his children, so he married Mimi and followed her whims. He had stood in front of Mimi, his hands lightly appraising her. This old man at the end of his career and this young woman at the start of her – what? Could she call herself an actress? Please God, more than a celebrity's child. Whatever were they doing together? Mimi got it, she understood why people wondered. But the magic hat the old comedian put on: how he made her laugh – at herself mostly. Her silly, selfish ways: her habit of eating all the nuts from the ice cream. All the swirls of caramel too. He made her look into the carton at the gouged mound, and asked, "Does this look appetizing to you, sweetheart? Anything like me?" She only had to be herself with Arnie and he was delighted. "You're allowed," he said. "Be your sweet, strange, selfish self."

Arnie Fine had her driven to the studio when she was in the pilot that did not get picked up. He didn't live to learn that the studio bumped it, but if Arnie were around he would say, "They didn't see you coming, doll." He said, "They're not ready for what you've got."

Now she walked out the sliding glass door and sat in the shallow end of the emptied pool. Some firm in charge – maybe the gang inside? – had set up folding chairs and a couple of card tables – and she watched as the aggressive old man maneuvered his walker to sit up close. She was glad the house was sealed, glad not to hear the noise inside until Donald came out to the terrace and said, "You're wanted."

After the house was dismantled, Donald Fine asked what she planned to do with the Mustang Arnie had left her buffed and ready at a downtown garage.

"Drive it?"

First date with Arnie they went from dipping sauces and luau-like drinks to the Dead Horse parking lot in Topanga Canyon where she played his Mustang. Oh, she had known from the start what an old gnome given to chuckling would like – a silly show-off who liked to make tight turns in empty lots. *Tight as my ass.* Arnie, he was fun. How was it he had had such dull children? Blame Ruthie? A mother cannot be held accountable for all the children's failings, for ignorance and bad taste. Donald Fine drove a chrome-heavy car he must have thought hot.

"I could use a drink," Donald said. And for some stupid reason – oh, vodka at Ricky's – she said yes, she could use a drink too and she canceled the car that was to take her to the hillside rental she'd found and buckled into Donald's car for the short drive to Ricky's. A vodka at Ricky's, yes, but as soon as the glacial-looking pool of clear fuel was set before her, Mimi knew she had made another bad decision. She saw the dusk ahead: on and on and so forth and then there was that time when . . . Donald told her how Arnie had left him at a party for some choice tail. Donald said he grew up on fumes of pussy. His father, that miserable fuck, funny-man, Arnie Fine . . . You should know, he said, but she didn't know and she didn't know and over two hours were junked until it came to this: she didn't know old movies, which made Donald really angry – "You never saw *Dinner at Eight*? I don't get you."

"You're not alone," she said, but all this to-do about an actress in a movie she hadn't seen?

"I'm saying – " Donald started.

"Quiet," she said. "I'm trying to hear what they're saying." A woman in the booth behind them, just a voice, said rather loudly, "How's she doing? She's a lot better. She's well enough to say her daughter's an asshole." There was more, but it was lost with Donald's blurted business, waving the bill, saying, "Will you look at this?"

Outside the restaurant, he said, "I mean, why go for a drink with someone if you're not going to talk?"

They said nothing more to each other until they were in the car, when Donald moaned how he couldn't take this sick shit.

"What did you and my dad ever have in common?"

"He didn't really like his kids and neither do I."

Despite the theatrical thunderhead rising above the mountains, Mimi drove toward it, drove into the desert with the top down at speeds equally dramatic. She wore cat's-eye sunglasses and a tied-on straw bonnet, the rim of which blatted in the wind. Desert-driving in a convertible! All of my cars have been convertibles — in her mother's voice — if only she could hear it, but Mimi's memory for any part of her mother was dismally approximate. To see the house again might help, but how to find it? A lot of people had cactus gardens. What made her think theirs was special? She passed through towns no bigger than beads and in between drove over eighty miles an hour. The clouds advanced in electric air. She looked up and felt the first large, sloppy drops of rain. The rain fell faster and she slowed up the car, pumped the brake, then braked hard and slewed onto the shoulder. She got the top up but not before it wet the dash; yet for all the water that fell from the sky – first the pockety sound, puffs of dust, then a downpour – the desert floor only steamed when it was over, hardly wet.

For her mother the desert was home. Sabine Agard – her mother's real name and no one in Hollywood had ever suggested she change it – was born in Algiers. Her first language was French and her accented English came out haltingly and often sounded like a small cry. She was very tiny; she wore a size four and a half shoe and size zero clothes. It didn't take a lot to kill her. Mimi thought if she could find the house, Sabine's troubled spirit might talk to her without talking to her as when they watched the dramas of fiery clouds dissipate in the desert sky, and Sabine warned Mimi in the very way she watched that men were dangerous.

Mimi bought water at the gas station and held the bottle against her face and considered the journey: how many hours out of LA, and here already. Now what? She bought a map and studied it – Culp, Canyon, Sweetbush – in hopes she might find the street. Then find the house, commune with Sabine, figure out the future. It didn't surprise her then that a man should step up to ask what she was looking for and might he help? His name was Zorn; he was from LA but he had a home in the desert. An attractive woman waited in the front seat of a Mercedes convertible although Mimi's Mustang was better.

Mimi said she was looking for a house she had lived in a long time ago. She couldn't remember the street, but the house was unusual, at least to her, then, a girl not quite twelve. The house she remembered didn't look like a house but like a pile of rusted salvage welded together. The cactus garden was dressed in stone.

He couldn't help her there, he said, and he was sorry and so was she.

The Indian who sold her the map at the convenience store didn't know the area either. He hauled up words in his heavy accent – was everyone in the desert from somewhere else? – and dropped them at her feet until, tired, he simply ceased to speak. At the Best Western the man at the front desk told Mimi the house had probably been swallowed up by the Bottlebrush development, and he showed her the way. She got herself a room, then drove out to find Bottlebrush and off Bottlebrush, an unpaved road. She remembered that much. No other houses nearby, but now how strange it was to see house after house of what she sort of remembered and the same stone cactus gardens, some with corroded ornaments, tin roadrunners and jack-rabbits and sunflowers – the sunflowers especially out of place. They had a pool, she remembered, ordinary, small. Once a photographer got access to the desert house and took photos of their mother stepping into the pool. In the photograph, her breasts were blurred. Her mother's former publicist and friend, Estelle, had given Mimi this photo, and others, at the memorial service, saying, "You may not want to look at these now." And for a long time Mimi didn't look; for a long time, she was angry at her mother.

At the end of a washboard road, Mimi found a house that seemed alike enough although its remembered welded quality had been altered somehow, whitewashed or stuccoed – something. A garage as charmless as a storage shed was now attached to the house, if this was the house, and she thought it was or it might be, given that it was the last house at the end of a long, rough road. The bucket chairs were gone, also the cacti. The desert looked the same from any angle, but the garden was just stone now, a terrible white in the light that had followed the storm. Mimi knocked at the front door but no one answered. She looked through a window and saw a churning gray as if the house were filled with water. She was about to knock again when a rattling car pulled roughly into the drive and nosed the garage. A woman in a sleeveless jean jacket opened the door. The woman's long arms were loose, all the fat tented near the elbow. She wore white tennis shoes; her legs were greenly varicosed. "I hope you're not here about my son."

"No."

"I've told the authorities all I know. I don't know where he is."

"No," Mimi said. "I'm here because I think I used to live here." This already seemed impossible.

"I doubt it, sweetie," the woman said, and Mimi was on the verge of agreeing.

"It would have been in the mid-nineties?"

The woman regarded her house with an appraising expression as if someone had offered her a lot of money for it. "Whyn't you come in and see?" She took out two bags of groceries from the backseat and Mimi followed her into the house. "Look familiar?" the woman asked. Her name, she told Mimi, was Dora Wozack. She was putting big cans of tomato juice into the kitchen cupboard. "Recognize anything?"

"No," Mimi said. "Not really." Already she had forgotten the woman's name.

"You looking up all the old places?"

Mimi knew this was not the house but once the jug of Stoli was out of the bag, she didn't want to leave. People came to the desert to dry out or drink, smoke or get spiritual, and this woman had the shape of a drinker. They drank from crystal quilted jars from when the woman, whose name Mimi still could not remember, made and sold prickly-pear jelly. "I had me quite a business for a while," she said, "then my husband died and Dean, that's my son, got crazier." Mimi waited for her to say more, but she didn't; instead, the woman asked about Mimi's car, how old it was and when she got it. Learning the car was a gift, she said, "Someone sure liked you."

"My husband," Mimi said.

"You look too young to be married."

"Well, I was. He died."

"I'm sorry," she said. "Accident?"

"Heart attack," Mimi said. "He was older."

"God, girl, I hope he was really old."

"Sixty-nine."

"How old are you?"

"Twenty-eight."

"My son's age," the woman said; "Dean," and just as she said his name, the son, the mean Dean, slammed his way into the kitchen with a gun and shot his mother in the face. Then he saw or seemed to see Mimi. He looked at her with no expression and what thoughts she couldn't even guess at though she made no effort to move or to speak before he turned the gun on himself. That fast. Mimi sat mute, witness to the immediate deflation of the body – the bodies – shapeless in clothes on the instant turned loose in a kind of flesh melt. Brain and bone and blood splatter on her shirt, the table, the floor, the window, her shoes in a puddle.

This was the house all right.

"Don't say I didn't warn you." Mimi held out the dustpan full of potsherds and let her brother pass into what she had found for herself, more charm than room, which he approved of, an artist's studio or a gardener's shed on a larger property in the hills.

"So it's small," Stetson said, "but give me that," and he took the dustpan and told her to get dressed: "It's afternoon."

"Who knew?" Mimi said, and she left Stetson looking around for a counter or a kitchen and walking slowly through the heart of the shed, as she called it, with its illusion of space: high ceilings and tiny furniture meant for children – and Mimi looked like a child when she emerged from around a corner dressed.

"Cute outfit," he said. "But can we put the pieces in a bag?"

"You really think Crazy Glue will do it?"

Mimi weaved among the opened and unopened boxes on her way to the kitchen along the wall. From under the sink, looking for a bag, she admitted the pot was not the first thing she had broken since yesterday. "I'm undone," she said, and she vowed never to be in the middle of a move again if she could help it. Forget being wrenched from the Piro house itself, the movers had flayed her. Tough, dismissive, they plastic-wrapped objects senseless – the movers swung tape guns over box flaps with a flourish. They sounded like butchers rending flesh. "I was meant to oversee – red dots go to Donald, yellow to Patricia – but I couldn't stand to watch the rooms emptied. I felt sorry for the furniture." She said, "You know what makes me sad? Tossed-out sofas, sofas left on the curb for collection. Ours on Cochran, remember? We put it out after the yard sale and in the middle of the night someone hacked off her legs."

Was it really only bad luck that Mimi had found Dora Wozack in a house she thought was once their own?

"I did think it was and then I didn't," Mimi said, and, "Now I'm here and I'm glad you've come." She led her brother around the house. Dora Wozack's house was certainly bigger. Dora Wozack in the kitchen, yukking over a quilted jar of vodka, took off her baseball cap and her hair was hardly there, more a gray reflective surface like brittlebush in summer, and Dora Wozack, like the shrub, waiting it out in the oven of old age. "My breasts are still my own," she had said, and they swayed, those big jolly breasts, when she leaned over to refill Mimi's glass. It's the other parts that're trouble.

"Mother's house was at the end of a different road entirely," Stetson said.

"Am I surprised," Mimi said. "I can go only so close to what happened."

"You never talk about the son."

"Mean Dean," she said. She opened a kitchen drawer to nothing and saw the boxes around the kitchen island. Saltines on the counter, but why? She found a knife and a hard, discolored lime. This was the start of the sober life: slow and strange for being attended to until she forgot what she was after. "What did I mean to do?"

"Come in here and sit down," Stetson said. "I'm not thirsty. I don't need anything to drink. We'll unpack together, but first sit down. Talk to me."

"Dean," she said. What did she know about him but through the gummy sieve of social media and search engine hits on his part for what? She guessed guns, pussy, older pussy, cum shot, green crack. Dean was not attractive. He came with his mouth open – too many teeth and breathing through his nose, his head unnaturally narrow as if it had been caught in a vise.

He came with his hard birth and nasty childhood, the frogs he shot with a BB gun, the cats he blew up with explosives. Several men stood in for fathers, one of them abused him with a hanger for which Dean blamed his mother. You bitch! Police statements, nursing records, court documents, he came with catalogs of officialese for a disturbed young man with a gun, a man dressed in gun colors, dark tattoos, and the blare of angry men on the radio, the TV, the street – Mimi could mash the killers together, all scars, bullying piercings, and bad breath.

But Dean can't shut his mouth!

Still he comes on at night some nights. He comes on bellowing, bellowing to his mother. "Hard to forget," Mimi said, then fell back against the couch relieved to have lived through it. "Thank God, you're here," she said.

Stetson leaned against her, bumped shoulders before he fell back into the couch. He talked about a time when he was still living in the Hills with their father and whoever else was taking care of him then – he was eleven – and he got into an aluminum foil fix. He took rolls of foil from the kitchen and no one ever complained or asked why, what was he doing with it, but they bought more. He was making an army. His stash took up half his closet – forts, figures, knives. He used most of the foil to make ammunition, aluminum bullets the size of golf balls he liked to whap off the upstairs porch at night, batting his threats with a badminton racket into the dark canyon, whooping and hoping to startle. Some dumb idea of fun when their father was away and the staff were in their quarters and quiet.

"Forget about that crazy Dean," Stetson said, and shoved himself off the couch, then pulled Mimi to her feet, helped her unpack. He used a box cutter on boxes she had walked around for days, and when she asked him about the box cutter, he explained he was leaving it with her. He'd brought her an essential toolkit, a householder's helper – hammers, nails, that sort of shit. "I was pretty sure you wouldn't have much more than scissors." He said, "I've made you smile."

He made her easy was how she thought of it. He enabled her to hear the satisfying thump of a well-made drawer sliding shut.

In the midst of Mimi's quaint kind-of scrapbook life, taking her old dog's ashes with her from place to place didn't seem so odd. And the small house suited Mimi; at least that is what Stetson told her. He took up the water she offered.

"In Jane Austen, first cousins marry, did you know that?" And when he didn't answer, she said, "I'd like to find someone like you."

"Or someone like Arnie."

"Or like Arnie," she said. "Made my life larger. Like living with a pet very comfortably, which isn't to say the pet wouldn't growl – he did. He bit or he nipped and he had his way on every outing: where we went, how we ordered, if he thought we deserved dessert. 'The force of his will could turn a slab of sidewalk into a gravestone.' That's not my line," she said.

"I didn't think it was."

"Arnie could be intense. He was dark."

"Our father thought so."

"But why can't Dad admit I might have been happy most of the time?"

"A friend of a friend of a friend – all gossip, whatever he heard."

And maybe her father was right about Arnie's interests – the rumors were out there. Besides, so many clichés about comedians prove true. The lonely childhood, for instance, and the solace found in movies. Family poverty that made Arnie laugh: the fire escape in their Brooklyn apartment was a rope tied to a radiator, and they often ate shoes for dinner. *Gedempte brust* his mother called it – a bad cut of meat roasted unrecognizable unless the eyelets of a dead man's shoes from Goodwill got stuck in your teeth. "Ma," Arnie said. The indomitable woman who hated her brother and famously served his family – all seven of them – a bag of chips still in the bag, a large bottle of soda and Dixie cups, the kind the dentists use. Help yourself! Dig in!

"Ma! How could she be so mean and me so nice, huh?"

Two o'clock sun when they lay together on the bleached teak chairs, and Arnie reached out and lightly touched her shoulder. A puffed sound, relief, a laugh, and then her name, "Mimi." After a while he said, "I've got a driver for you for tomorrow's shoot."

And so he did, and early the next morning, in the muddy in-between hour reserved for crises, Mimi Deminthe eased into the town car that took her to Paramount Studios where she played a ditzy girl on set who said such things as "What does insufficient funds mean?"

Later, on the way home, she slept in the backseat of the town car while the driver took the jolts of traffic to the famous house. And not until early evening did she walk through it to the back and the glass sliding door, beyond which were the pool and Arnie. The heart attack had happened around one, but the coroner's report, more exact, was a sour reminder that no one in this life is so twinned as to feel the other's exit. No heart-pinch burn for her in the moment when Arnie died. When Arnie's heart clenched, Mimi was shaking max-energy mix-max into a smoothie on stage 30 at Paramount.

Only the day before, poolside in the afternoon, her hand over Arnie's warm hand, so deeply ridged and knuckled her fingers fit between – only the day before. Why had she walked distractedly through it? Why hadn't they stayed in the bleached teak chairs laughing?

"One Jewish pirate says to another, 'You know how much they're charging for sailcloth these days? I can't afford to pillage and rape anymore.'"

Jokes – his own or someone else's.

More than once he said, "I'm sorry about my kids — they were loyal to Ruthie and right to be loyal."

In one of the obituaries, Arnie was described as stunned "by his implausible good fortune."

Was she, Mimi Deminthe, a part of that good fortune?

"You forgot who you were for a while," Stetson said, "living in that abstract painting. The name makes it sound famous, but the Piro house was bereft of life, Mimi, it was barren . . . rusty water, old pipes, old tiles."

"I wanted to go up in smoke in it, get on the pyre with Arnie."

"I love the way you throw yourself into everything." He smiled at her. "Little sister, when did you start wearing baby doll dresses with blue jeans?"

"Since I decided to act my age."

A friend of Stetson's made beautiful clay pots that were glazed to look like pewter, and Stetson encouraged Mimi to replace the broken pot with another, maybe one from Wyatt's studio.

"My brother said you made beautiful pots and that I might find something."

*   *   *

The next time she saw Stetson she was still at a loss. "I haven't had a drink since . . . oh, last week?" She said, "I see Dora Wozack dying every day." She said, "I remember I wanted a shirt like hers, cowboy cut with snap buttons. Dora said she loved an afternoon vodka and then sleep. Fuck dinner. The problem was, she said, she got up after midnight and rummaged through the kitchen for crap to eat. M&M's with peanuts. Somehow that was funny: I was laughing. Dora Wozack said, 'My son's troubled,' or maybe, 'My son's trouble.' It could have been 'in trouble.'"

"You've got to get out of the house," Stetson told her.

"I am," she said. "I do," she said. "But why should I?" Their mother's mother lived in a wet cottage that smelled of cheese; she rarely left it, which accounted for the smell or so their mother thought. And their mother? – she never went beyond the cactus garden in the desert house, whereas they had gone far and wide. More than once, Stetson and Mimi had wandered into the cholla forest and played at being lost.

"I got us out of the desert," Mimi said.

"That time the police came to the door?" Stetson asked though he knew the answer already – they had come for Sabine Agard, dead at thirty-nine. And Mimi had nothing to do with that greasy guy with the rubber nose and clown shoes, impatient, bored, come to make them laugh on Mother's birthday, last birthday. Their father sent the comedian.

The man who came to their mother's house with the pool hose and sucked up the dead squirrels was expected.

"He used a net, Mimi!"

"Really?"

But their father that time was a surprise. He came to the house when the sky was an uplifting blue. He came with a gift of jewel-shoes so minuscule their mother's glass foot just fit them. Then the breakage at night: glasses, plates, windows, bottles of expensive perfume. Pure Hollywood! In the morning, he was gone, and not long after, their mother, forever.

Mimi said. "Let's find another topic, please."

He rapped his knuckles against his forehead. "Okay," he said. "I remember where I am now," and he stood up, rocked his shoulders, leaned back, stretched.

Just to watch him felt good, and then she was tugged by the hand off the couch and taking small steps after her brother out of the shed and into the just-right night of Los Angeles in . . . ? Let's say it was May in the first decade of the hardly promising twenty-first century, and a white stucco wall, corsaged in bougainvillea and lit up by the moon, enticed them downhill a long way past gated properties to a wider road, then down that road and across it on the other side to the lookout onto the sparkle that was the city and what lay before them at the liftoff of another beginning, which feeling they would experience again, until decades shrank to pieces of colored stone, mosaics unexpected and unfitted yet shellacked together and made to glow alike in recollection so that all she had known of love and the end of love could be summoned and summed up in a ceiling pinked in sulfurous light.

THE HEDGES

The woman who had just been identified as attached to Dick Hedge looked pained by the clotted, green sound of her little boy's breathing, an unwell honk that did not blend in with the sashaying plants and beachy-wet breeze of the island. "Jonathan," she said, and she spoke into the little boy's ear and made sounds to soothe him, though he would not be soothed. The little boy twisted in her arms to be released. He leaned as far back and away from her as he could, which the mother said hurt. "Don't!" she said. "I can't hold you. Jonathan!" She said, "Will you please hold still?" Luckily for her, she had a husband. Dick Hedge helped his wife into the waiting golf cart, then took his place on the other side of Jonathan who, surprised or tired, sat very still for the ride.

Probably, they did not want to miss the sunset, for they were not long in their cabana. Of course, Lolly Hedge had seen plenty of these sunsets before; she had been to many islands actually. Aruba, Curaçao, Saint John, Saint Thomas, Saint Croix, Little Cayman. Her uncle owned a lot of land in Little Cayman, so the vacation there had been the best trip of them all; like visiting the family compound – everything was free. The best trip, yes. "Except for this one," she said in an obligatory voice or a sad voice or a tired voice – it was hard for anyone listening in to tell. The voice – small, but husky – how to describe it? Lolly's voice was Lolly's most distinguished feature. The woman in front of her smiled, beguiled (no doubt by the voice), and told Lolly that the black beans were very piquant and that she, Lolly, should try them. Dick stood just behind his wife holding Jonathan and explaining the food to the boy although the difference between pineapple and mango did not seem to interest Jonathan. Besides, the poor little chap was on this pink medicine, this viscid antibiotic that he often gagged on and which left him sleepy and without an appetite. "Jonathan has been sick for weeks," Lolly said to the woman in front of her. "One of the reasons we decided to come here was to get well."

Lolly was right about the medicine's irritating side effects; Jonathan fussed at dinner and could be mollified only with apple juice, which he drank in a sore slump in the corner of a basket seat. Sometimes Jonathan wagged the bottle by the nipple held between his teeth. He watched his father eat, but whenever he looked at his mother, he whimpered. "Jonathan," she said, sounding exhausted again or sad. "Jonathan, please. Let Mommy be."

The Hedges did not stay for dessert. By then, the sun had set, and the night sky's show was blinking on quickly. A greater darkness amid the foliage squeaked notes, very pretty. In his father's arms again, Jonathan cried and leaned out toward his mother to carry him, but the way was too steep. Lolly did not look at the boy, and she did not speak to him. His father, carrying him, was silent while Jonathan cried against Dick's shoulder and looked back at his trailing mother and never once looked to the nest of cabanas where they were going up and up a hillside of jutting verandas in thin shrubbery.

Lolly must have cribbed the boy in pillows on the bed and slept to one side of him because the next morning Dick was at the front desk arranging for the rental of a crib; there were no other children in sight, and the hotel was not prepared for them.

"At the beach," the concierge said. "Everybody."

Yes, yes, yes, Dick had a wife already there. She was watching from under the palms as her little boy threw sand. Sand gritted his mouth and his bubbly nose. Even the juice in his bottle looked silted. "I give up," Lolly said to her husband, but her husband walked right past her toward Jonathan, making noises of surprise to see him. Dick dropped on his knees in front of the boy and used the long hem of his shirt to clean Jonathan's face, saying, "Hold still," but the boy kept tossing his head until what his father was doing hurt Jonathan, and he cried.

"Oh, God!" The parents sighed to see Jonathan crab his way to the water.

"Oh, God." This time it was Lolly speaking. "Damn it, Dick —" and she made as if to lift herself out of the web chair as Dick hopped over the already hot sand toward Jonathan.

"Ouch, ouch, ouch, ouch, ouch," he clowned, and when he caught up to Jonathan he urged the little boy toward the water, but Jonathan did not want to get wet now and held back, frightened. "I'm going," his father said; nevertheless, when he let go of Jonathan's hand, the little boy cried out, "No!" His voice carried, or so it seemed to his mother as she looked down the beach to where the other early risers lay, and Lolly thought she saw them grimace in her direction. "Dick," she called, "carry him."

Dick reacted slowly and calmly or it might have been that he was simply tired, but he did not rush. He tossed his shirt in the direction of his wife and picked up the crying child and carried him into the water, taking care to keep Jonathan out of the water, putting his own wet hands on the boy's knees and moving his mouth against the boy's face and trying, it seemed, very patiently trying, to get the boy used to it, but Jonathan kept whimpering and holding out his arms for his mother, so Dick said, "All right," and he plunged with the boy into the unfurling wave. He paddled backward into the foam. "Oh!" Any one of them said that. "Oh!" Dick was laughing and his wife was scolding from afar, "What are you . . ." and the little boy was crying and coughing up water.

"It's too cold, Dick!" Lolly stood in the water now with her arms outstretched. "Give him to me." But Dick kept hold of the little boy and bobbed and laughed and seemed smoothly confident he could jolly his son into ease. Lolly, at the shore, kept calling, "Mommy's going to get you," and when she did at last take hold of Jonathan, the small cage of bones that was his chest heaved, so that his mother held him closely and let the boy use her as a bib to rub himself warm against and to clean his face of slaver.

"Someone will be tired," Lolly said as they walked off the beach, but in the end Jonathan's vexations did not make him tired. No mid-morning nap for this boy and not much of a nap after lunch. Usually the medicine made him sleepy, but on their first day at the resort Jonathan stood in the rickety crib the management had found for the family and shook its bars. That was how Lolly described the rout of naptime. She had tried to go on reading on the terrace. She did not look behind her at the swelling curtains; she did not respond to the tuneless xylophone of his bottle banged against the crib slats. Let him rattle, let him cry. Who was there near enough to hear him? They were farther up the mountain in a suite more exclusively pitched. Of course they had paid more.

But who wanted to know how much more? They didn't have the most expensive. They didn't have the version with the private lap pool. But the cost of things did not interest Lolly. What she wanted to know was how long did motherhood last? After the noisy beginning of his nap, Jonathan had plumped down onto the mattress. He was making little bubble sounds, and it seemed he was falling asleep, so. So? What was it that made him stand up and cry?

But that was why they were here now, so early, at the pool. The familiar woman from last night's dinner said oh, yes, indeed, she could certainly understand, the boy was . . . well, just look at the boy, so alive, the way he reached for his mother!

Lolly said to the boy, "Daddy will take you."

Sadly, the pool was not as blue as it was in the brochures. On her uncle's island the water was so bright Lolly didn't dare look at it directly.

"Dick," she called out to her husband, "don't you want sunglasses?"

Dick and Jonathan were sitting on the steps into the pool; no one was swimming. Lolly, just behind them on a long chair, was getting sleepy. The whiteness of things – the canvas umbrellas and cabanas, the pool's paved edge – stunned the plants still. The boy and his father were silent. The boy sat in water to his waist and floated his arm on the surface of the water; the father's face was water in a glass, without expression. He said nothing to Lolly's voice, so his wife shut her eyes and woke alone in the shade.

When had they left?

"A long time ago," the nearest guest said.

Itchy, sunburned – Lolly walked unsteadily toward the white glare beyond the palm trees, but when she saw Dick, she turned back for her room before he saw her.

(Later, after the accident, a guest remembered seeing Lolly walking up the hill toward the cabana. She was crying. She was crying and unsteady and tripped on a step. The guest said he would have helped but that Lolly was too far away from him, and she was in a hurry and didn't seem to want help. The way her body swiped past staff and guests, he could see her disdain for them.

"The young woman could be supercilious," said the woman who swam with Lolly some mornings.)

Jonathan, on the beach, gouged the sand with a shovel he held like a lance. His father fell asleep. No one saw the little boy walk off, although even Lolly claimed she heard him, and knew he was lost. What crying!

*   *   *

"But I am," Lolly said. "We are," she insisted. She was standing in the buffet line at dinner. Her pert dress had bow-tied string straps and matched the flowers on her sandals. Washed hair, lipstick. Her pale skin was mesmeric and slick under the light of netted globes. Jonathan was not with them. He had been found, bathed, pajamaed: he was asleep. "Lucky us," Lolly said, and then the Hedges ate in silence.

Sometime in the night when the tree frogs had ceased to sing, a cry, followed by another, sounded on the hillside. It might have been a sound of pleasure or pained pleasure or something else; the cry was ambiguous. One of the guests thought it might have been the little boy, the only little boy – the only child – at the resort, but the little boy seemed better the next morning. He could walk; no one carried him into the breakfast room. Jonathan held his mother's hand, and he was subdued, even serene at the table. He sucked on a wedge of toast.

Dick and Lolly looked tired, but after breakfast they took off in a taxi to tour the island. They returned hours later, just after noon. Lolly hoisted herself from the taxi and walked off with her arms held out; she smelled of vomit. She walked quickly to her cabana. No lunch, no tea, no sunset cocktail for her – not even dinner.

"I hope your wife is not unwell," from someone who noticed Dick alone with Jonathan at a dark corner table. Dick said, no, Lolly was asleep, a long day with the baby. Dick said that if they were at home, Jonathan would be in bed.

And where was home?

In the middle of the country.

Nothing to be embarrassed about, the man said and looked on as Dick worried the boy's fingers apart to get hold of something speared and plastic. Jonathan fought for it, but once it was lost, he looked around and was distracted, expectant, hopeful as a dog for the next toy, and he got it: a slice of orange from Father's drink to suck on.

Again, in the night, there was a noise, but this time it did sound like a baby.

Lolly was a princess by her own admission; the noisiness of snowscapes, of snow falling or newly fallen, gave her headaches, so that island vacations were best. This was Jonathan's first such vacation, but Lolly confessed she had not considered the meaninglessness of travel for a two-year-old. Soft fruit with Cheerios was breakfast anywhere for Jonathan, and he smeared banana into his mouth and gooed his arms and the bib of his shirt.

Cereal stuck to him as it would to anything that oozed, and Lolly said she did not want to get near the boy. "Stay away from me," she said in a serious voice, but she smiled at the boy, so it seemed she was joking, and he reached for her again and she screamed. Hardly what had been heard on the hillside last night. Last night's screams had sounded astonished.

Did Lolly like her baby?

Lolly often fell asleep on the job so that whoever was still awake had to care for the little boy, but where was he, Jonathan?

Asleep, asleep.

After that day on the beach when the boy wandered away and discovered he liked the water, for a time at least liked it, on his own, after that day when the boy could have drowned, Dick and Lolly kept Jonathan on the terrace that trembled in the light through the split-leaf fans and flapping foliage. Jonathan played on the terrace with a local girl who saw to it that he was fed.

So Jonathan had a local nanny. How else to explain how blissfully empty-handed Lolly was. "Look at me," and she shut her eyes in mid-sentence and fell asleep on the beach.

When she woke, she waved at her husband. "Good luck chasing fish!" she called out to him. Dick was on the ocean for so long – all afternoon – that Lolly went to the dock in search of him, not worried, but curious:

and there he was on the boat. There was Dick on the big and tipsy vessel that slowed to the dock. They did not have a camera between them, but the resort took a picture of Dick as he stood next to his fish.

Had Lolly ever heard of a wahoo? For that was what Dick had caught and ordered grilled for dinner.

The dinner could have been photographed, too, but they didn't have a camera. Lolly had seen this scenery before, and Jonathan was sick. She didn't want a picture of a sick little boy. No, when Jonathan was well, then they would buy a camera. For now, for Lolly, it was nice, a treat, a real pleasure to sleep in the sun without worry. It was enough. Shells, shell jewelry, decorated mirrors and flowerpots and smoky perfumes, coconut creams and coconut heads and apothecary jars of sea glass and colored sand were so much village junk. She liked to be empty-handed.

Another night Dick sat at dinner alone.

"I hope the family is okay," said the concierge when Dick asked for a doctor he might call in case. But yes, they were okay. His wife was only tired, and the little boy was happiest eating toast with his mother. The little boy was fine, yes. Dick had nothing more to talk about. He wandered into a daze and ate alone and silently, and after dinner he walked the beach. Dick Hedge, a young man with a tired face, sipping a foamy cocktail. He had another cocktail at the bar and still another when the dancing began. He swiveled in his seat to watch everyone partnered. Later when he weaved his way through the dancers, the music was louder but some of his words – don't . . . why . . . can't – carried and a dancer looked after him: why was the young man so often alone?

After the second day at the resort they penned the little boy in the terrace of their cabana. Lolly said Jonathan just loved Cecilia. Cecilia was courtesy of the resort. Her mother was on the staff. Heavy, brown, robustly pretty, Cecilia looked alert enough for a girl, but she was twelve, so was it any wonder? Cecilia and Jonathan were on the terrace every day. She kept the sliding windows open so he could crawl from the terrace to the bedroom and around the bathroom and into the closets. Most of the cabanas on the hill were not large; the Hedges did not have the version with the pool.

The little boy was restless and one day he climbed onto the bed, then onto the tippy dresser chair, then onto the dresser. Cecilia laughed to tell Lolly how she had found Jonathan on the dresser, bumping against the reflection of himself in the dresser mirror, making faces.

Cecilia said, "He sure look like he feel something then."

* * *

The next day Lolly reported as much to the woman she called the Swimmer. Yes, Jonathan was better. Only one more day on the pink medicine, and wouldn't that be a relief. Then Jonathan might play freely in full sun. Then they could be like a family again. But no more golf! No, Dick would have to squeeze in the holes during naptime, and there would be no more mornings like this one for her. Lolly laughed and the familiar flowered cap nodded back. This woman, the Swimmer, was Lolly's clock. There before anyone else and swimming back and forth and back and forth, this woman held on to the edge of the pool and tried to kick, but her heavy lower body stayed below. She strained to kick and listened to Lolly.

"That's my morning," Lolly said to Dick on the patio at lunch when she was describing the Swimmer. At lunch on the patio, Lolly described the Swimmer's struggle in the water, the small splashes that were kicks. Lolly made a comparison between her life and the woman's swimming, the struggle to break the surface.

"Jesus," Dick said. He was not in the mood for Lolly's tireless, tiredly lyrical self-analysis. He was flushed; he had played poorly; he wanted a beer. "If that's how you feel," he said.

"My father told me . . ."

"Your father, your father . . . give me a break."

"I am finding it hard, Dick."

"Hard? What's hard, Lolly?" Dick called over the waiter and ordered his beer. "I know what you could make hard."

Someone at a nearby table overheard this last remark – or maybe all of the remarks – and coughed.

Lolly loudly pushed away from the table and stood up. "I hate this fucking place," she said to the cougher, and then she walked off in the direction of the beach.

(Later, after the accident, this squabble on the patio would be remembered by more than one other guest, and it wasn't the sound of Lolly's voice this time that made the impression. There were others, not just the cougher, who wondered why these two, so lovely and young and clearly comfortable if not rich, why they, with their pouty, pretty son, were so unhappy.

Why did Lolly frown so much?

Why was it Dick drank and drank alone?

Was it their little boy? Was it that they did not know what to do with their little boy? Why had they brought him if they meant to keep him out of sight and in the care of a girl who was clearly unequipped? Why had they selected this resort and not one geared for younger couples and their children?

These were some of the questions some people asked after the accident.)

What was no accident but bad luck was the direction Lolly walked in after the incident on the patio because after she left Dick at the table she walked away from the resort, down the strip of beach that came to rock, and then over the rock – she scraped her legs climbing – to the wilder beach growth that scratched. She walked through this brittle, scratchy, wild stuff to the road and continued to walk toward what might become a village. But she never discovered a village, because after more than an hour, Dick came up behind her in a taxi. He opened the door and beckoned her inside. "Please," he said. "Something has happened."

Lolly knew enough to get in and that was when he told her.

If she had walked to the cabana instead of toward nothing, the boy might have been saved.

But who could blame the girl Cecilia? Cecilia was a girl, and Jonathan was a restless, fully mended little boy. One minute he was in the bedroom watching TV with Cecilia, and the next, he was gone to the terrace. Jonathan, the climber, climbed onto the terrace chair and then onto the table and then over the railing. Jonathan fell more than twenty feet to the rock path below the terrace. He fell and on the instant died. He fell over the railing and cracked his skull and many other bones that gave him shape.

(Later, the resort guest chorus ooohed but stayed away and mostly quiet. "We're on vacation," the guests said. Only Lolly's morning friend, the Swimmer, came forward and saw the couple off. The Swimmer, a woman acquainted with loss, saw the Hedges' sad departure and thought now Lolly Hedge had more than a musical voice; now she had a story, for which in time she might say she was thankful.)

SPECIES OF SPECIAL CONCERN

On the subject of plant names Bob Cork was indifferent: the common names for things were commonly changing. "Call her what you like," Bob Cork said, so Dan looked into the orange-yolk bell of a quaintly named daylily – "Button Box" – and considered its strong, heavy stem.

"Let's call her 'Nancy Cork,'" he said.

"There's an idea!"

"Which direction did she go in, your wife?"

Bob Cork pointed toward the north meadow and a view of not so much land as sky – all promise for the lepidopterist. "She's got the ATV now," he said, "an off-road vehicle. Four-wheel," he said. The ATV meant she could drive over any terrain and add to her life list. Nancy Cork, famous as a sighter for species of special concern. "Spicebush swallowtail," Bob Cork said. "Not seen since 1934. She saw him last year and she hopes to see him again." Bob Cork, a lean, hempen, homiletic man, worn as his old jeans – duct-taped sandals, corkscrew ponytail – told Dan that the "Grisley"-model ATV he had recently bought his wife, despite her protests at the expense, was top of the line. "I told her I want a bank full of memories, not a bank full of money."

Bob Cork used the same line to describe how he had talked Nancy Cork into a spring vacation in the U.S. Virgin Islands. Only the flying was hard. They hadn't expected a pat-down at security and tried to explain what was inside Nancy that made the machines bleep, but those TSA folks, man, they'd gone ahead and made her cry. Nancy's arm was swollen to the size of a ham to begin with. Worst part of the trip, really.

Bob Cork, in a ditch again in one of his stories, worried his mouth like a toothless man.

Dan wondered at him. Why hadn't Bob Cork bundled his wife in pillows and throws and kept her comfortable through the winter? But he wanted to sozzle tropical drinks while he stood in water to his waist.

Bluest water they'd ever seen. "Like blue diamonds," Bob Cork said.

And every part of Nancy Cork smarting in it, no doubt.

Dan looked out at the tired nursery: slugs on the ligularia and mildewed phlox; hostas exhausted and bee balm ruffed as fighting cocks.

"My phlox is mildewed, too," he said.

Bob Cork said, "Nursery's always been Nancy's, you know. And I've got the twin grandkids now and the little horses to take care of." Bob Cork held up a daylily, set it down, and said: "Nancy's stopped treatment." Then he lifted up another "Nancy Cork," many-stemmed and hardy, and set it in the wagon at Dan's nodding assent.

"Great," Dan said, meaning the plant, of course, but he saw Bob Cork's eyes wobble, and he looked away at the daylily in the wagon and for a time was respectfully silent. Dan said, "If you could find me one more like this one."

Dan was sure Nancy Cork prized, above all, her privacy in pain. Howling was something to be done in the wilderness. They had a shared love of plants, which translated into a view of nature as brutal and final – few plants die well, most go out grotesque. Best cut them down. Dan knew that if Nancy Cork were here she would hide her blown-up parts and carry on – she was carrying on. Over twenty acres of fields and woods for her to track the everyday as much as the rare and endangered, the cabbage whites and mustards, orange sulphurs, clouded sulphurs, little sulphurs or little yellows. Nancy Cork was adding to her life list. She was impressing new paths on the meadows and the scruffier places with her Grisley ATV four-wheeler.

"Yes," Dan said, "that daylily, and one more like it."

Bob Cork had a good eye for vigorous plants but no genuine interest in them. He was a birder, a retired high school biology teacher, a breaker of little horses, and – most important of all – a grandpa to twin grand-kids. "It's a lot of work and with Nancy's plants," Bob Cork said.

Dan had never seen the grandkids, but he had seen the little horses in the barn, dull stubby ponies, furred like buffalo, rough bangs, tiny eyes – unpettable. *Our grandkids can't stop loving on them!* Bob Cork's refrain was hard to credit. Dan was sure Nancy Cork didn't like pets. She expressed no affection for the cats sprung out from under plants in ghost attacks and feints. She said nothing about dogs. Wolflike dogs made piteous sounds down the road, but at Nancy Cork's Hidden Gardens, all was butterflies and plants and birds. Such interests fitted neatly into the story Dan had in his head while other hobbies of hers still surprised him, threw him off, made him think he knew nothing about her. Ballroom dancing, for one. Envision Bob and Nancy Cork, lean and fat, a Jack Sprat from the rhyme with his nuggety wife doing the Lindy Hop, fox-trot, rumba, and waltz. Admittedly, the Cajun-style rhythm two-step, newer to the repertoire, was a challenge, but Bob Cork liked to say, "It ain't whatcha do, it's the way that you do it," a platitude that left him a lot of room on the dance floor.

Had Nancy Cork ever made a face – even a small one – then or at any time when she and Dan and Bob Cork were a threesome in the driveway, and Bob Cork was droning on while she totted up the bill and Dan packed the plants in his car? Bob Cork on tax codes and piss repellent, climate change, health insurance, and no one responding – not so much as a grunt.

Nancy Cork's face under a bucket-hat brim. Did Dan know her face – had he ever known it? And now, now when she so clearly had turned away from them all, did he remember it correctly? Her confiding sidelong look at him with the greenhouse as background, had he imagined it? Nancy Cork, slightly crooked upturned nose, soft cheeks, sly mouth, had he made her up over the course of every summer?

Years ago, Bob Cork had let out that his wife didn't sleep well in summer heat and some nights sat on the porch and played her accordion. The accordion! To think of it – and Dan did think of it. No one around for miles and miles to hear her. Nancy Cork seated on the outdoor glider, wearing only a short apron and the shield of her accordion as she shifted her old-fashioned generous fanny and leaned into her pleasure. Sometimes he put her in high heels with ice-pick toes, black patent-leather stilettos on a gardener who wore clogs and loose clothes. He lacked imagination – he lacked.

"How long has she been out in the field today?" he asked when Nancy Cork had been out in the field or at the doctor's office on every one of his several visits. He had not seen her all summer and the summer before

65

that once, only once, between treatments, hopeful of remission. *How long has she been out?* Idiot, yet he fumbled forward, "I'm sad to miss her. But there's a daylily in her name and maybe . . ." It was too fatuous to even suggest a next summer; still he said it, "Maybe next summer . . ."

Bob Cork bobbed up on his springboard knees, a dancer, a tall and gangly figure, Bob Cork was about to lose his wife, and he blinked like a newborn in the light, eyes seeming oily, unready, dismayed.

"Summer's over, you say," Bob Cork said; "That happened fast." He pulled the wagon alongside the two of them as they walked back to the potting shed and the parking lot.

After a while, Dan said yes, the summer was over for him. He was ready and however hesitantly he might have added *to go back to Boston,* he *was* ready, but for the going back itself. The return trip meant driving away in the dark, well before dawn, so as not to see what he was leaving behind in Maine, which was his garden, a pride, a comfort, a habit – an obsession. He lacked the vocabulary for it, and anyway only Nancy Cork might understand him. They had talked plants before. It didn't matter that she had never come to see his garden – despite his open invitation, despite the garden's several appearances on the garden club tour – Nancy Cork knew what it was, she had always known what it was he would miss about Maine.

Dan flattened out the tarp in the back of the wagon for the daylilies and went on about the logistics of leaving his summer house as if it mattered to Bob Cork or anyone how early in the morning he had to leave or what lay ahead and was not arousing to look at: baked brick mill towns with their bristle of church spires, clock towers, smokestacks – all dead. There was that ahead of Boston and what felt like the rest of his life –

How could he think of next summer without her – no matter there had been a summer, this summer, without her: Nancy Cork. Nancy Cork, one of the gray ladies of Maine was how Dan's late wife Marion, ever blond, might have described her. They never had a chance to meet. Besides, Marion's enjoyment of gardening had come chiefly from deadheading, pruning, and spraying for mildew and rust. As for the Japanese beetles, so ruinous to the rugosas, she liked to point a can of Raid up close, cover them in poison, and watch the lurid fornicators drop – hah! Marion, a decade gone, and in that time, he'd bought and planted another half acre. He had found Hidden Gardens and Nancy Cork's plants. He sometimes thought it terrible how easy it was to get on, and he began to share these thoughts, but Bob Cork skipped the rail of their conversation and said, "No looking back." For him it was day to day. "All's I do is hope there'll be another," he said.

Dan said, "There will be."

"I mean for her," Bob Cork said, and the air went out of Dan's scenery.

"Oh."

The little *oh* was all that was left of Dan's story, the one that played out in his head about a husband with a ponytail and his purposeful, dying wife. As far as Dan was concerned, Nancy Cork was a woman needful and deserving of more love than her self-absorbed husband could give, whereas he, he could give . . . *oh.*

He could not put a name to it or perhaps ever find it again.

A HAPPY RURAL SEAT OF VARIOUS VIEW: LUCINDA'S GARDEN

They met Gordon Brisk on a Friday the thirteenth at the Clam Box in Brooklin. They pooh-poohed the ominous signs. The milky stew they ate was cold – so what? They were happy. They were at sea; they were at the mess, cork-skinned roughs in rummy spirits, dumb, loud, happy. And they really didn't have so much to say to each other. They were only a few months married and agreed on everything, and for the moment nearly everything they did – where and how they lived – was cheap or free. They expected gifts at every turn and got them.

So it was at the Clam Box on a Friday night – lime pits along the rim of the glass, Pie feeling puckered – when Gordon Brisk introduced himself as a friend of Aunt Lucinda's from a long time ago. Nick said he had seen Gordon's paintings, of course. And Gordon said, "I'm not surprised."

Gordon told a story that included Aunt Lucinda when she was their age. There were matches in it and another young woman who almost died. Aunt Lucinda in the story was the same – all love, love, love and this time for Gordon – and as for Gordon himself? He held up his hands. His hands had been on fire. He said, "Just look at these fuckers," and they did. They looked and looked. The hands should have scared them, but they were drunk and sunburned and happy. They were glad, they insisted, glad to have met him. "Our first famous person," Pie said after the after-dinner drinks when she and Nick were in the Crosley driving home.

Pie was driving, too fast; she was saying how she loved those amber-colored, oversweet drinks, the ones with a floating orange slice and a cherry. She had had too many, so was it any surprise she hit something? She hit something large and dark, but fatally hesitant. The Crosley, a gardener's minicar, had no business on a public road, but Pie had wanted to drive it. The Crosley was a toy, yet whatever Pie hit hobbled into the woods, dragging its broken parts.

Home again and in their beds, Pie and Nick took aspirin and turned away from each other and slept. Next morning – frictive love – and then as usual in the garden, Aunt Lucinda's garden, the famous one, a spilling-over, often photographed, seacoast garden. The garden was how they lived for free. They were the caretakers of an estate called The Cottage. Some cottage! Why would Aunt Lucinda leave this paradise, they asked, but she had told them. His name was Bruno and his wealth exceeded hers. The villa he owned in Tuscany was staffed. "Everything there is arranged for my pleasure," so Aunt Lucinda said.

Gordon had said, "Scant pleasure." He had said, "I'll tell you pleasure. The killing kind." And then to almost everyone at the Clam Box bar, he described his wife: shoeblack hair and pointy parts. That cunt was the source of the fire, or so he had said at the Clam Box. "I was fucking around," was what Gordon had said, "but who wouldn't?"

They were untested, Pie and Nick. They were newly everything; and now here they were caretakers for a summer before the rest of life began, and on this morning, as on so many mornings, the cloudless sky grew blue, then bluer. White chips of birds passed fast overhead, and the water was bright; they looked too long at its ceaseless signals and at noon they zombied to it. They let the waves assault them and knock them back to shore. Sand caught in all the cracked places, and it felt good to take off their suits and finger it out. Up the beach they lay directly on the sand; they dozed, they woke, they brushed themselves off. They wanted nothing. They were dry and their suits were dry and, for a moment, warm against them, and they walked to the shore, walked along the shore and then into the water. They knew the water all over again. So went the afternoon in light – no clouds – whereas indoors was dark.

It was dark, but they ran through the mudroom toward the phone. They ran, and then they missed it. Who cared? They had the late afternoon before them.

They tended the garden. Nick and Pie, they watered the deep beds; they flourished arcs; they beaded hooded plants and cupped plants and frangible rues. They washed paths. The wet rock walls turned into gems. What a place this was! How could Aunt Lucinda's Bruno match it? Of course, the sunsets could be overlong if all they did was watch them, but they were distracted. The hot showers felt coarse against their sunburned skin and the lotion was cold. They put on pastel colors and saw their eyes in the mirror – another blue!

Another summer dusk, stunned by the sun's garish setting, they stood close to the grill and the radio's news. They were in love and could listen, horrified but untouched, to whatever the newscaster had to say. But the flamboyant infanticide accomplished with duct tape was too much. It had happened just north of them in the next and poorest county.

"Turn that off!" Nick said, and Pie did.

For them, nothing more serious than the dark they finally sat in with plates on their laps and at their feet melted drinks that looked dirty.

*   *   *

"Death: will it be sudden and will we be smiling? Will we know ourselves and the life we have lived?"

"Don't even think such things!"

But Pie did, and Nick did, too.

He said, "Think of something else," and Pie came up with Gordon.

Gordon at the Clam Box. His high color and his scribbled hair. The way he startled whenever they had swayed closer. Was he afraid he might be touched? But there were all those women. An actress they had heard of. A lot of other men's wives. Aunt Lucinda. "A beauty," was what he said of her. Cornelia Shelbey had been a girlfriend, too, until the Count swooped down. A prick, the Count. Cornelia Shelbey was a cunt.

"What are we?" they had asked.

"Conceited!"

Nevertheless, Gordon called them. The picnic was his idea. Mid-morning and already hot; the coast, a scoured metal, stung their eyes. Even as they drove against the wind, they felt the heat. There was no shade for a picnic. The tablecloth, held down with rocks, blew away. The champagne crinkled. The food they ate was salty or dry: no tastes to speak of. Nick wanted peanut butter and jelly on pink, damp bread. Instead here were cresses and colored crisps. Then the champagne began. Pie swallowed too much of an egg too fast and it hurt her throat.

Gordon said of Aunt Lucinda's Bruno, "The man's a fool. He knows nothing about art, but he lets people play with his money." Gordon picked at the knees of his loose khaki pants and what he found he flicked away into the sea grass. He asked, "How do you play with yours?"

They told him just how little they had.

"Too bad!" he said. "Poor you."

Pie washed her sticky hands in the cooler's melting ice. Gordon yawned. Then they all three pushed the picnic back into the basket, didn't bother to fold the tablecloth, drove home.

A storm the next day; the power thunked out. Nick and Pie still had headaches from the picnic – too much champagne and whatever they had drunk afterward – so they took more aspirin. They napped; they looked at the sky; they shared a joint, and they knocked around in bed and felt rubbed and eased when they were finished. It was quiet in The Cottage except for the sound of the rain. They talked about money until they made themselves thirsty. Downstairs on the porch they saw Gordon in the garden under the tent of a golf umbrella.

Gordon said he'd walked all the way from the village to them, walked in the rain to get sober. "Last night," he said sadly. He shut the umbrella and sat on the porch with his head in his ruined hands.

So they lit the fat joint rolled against the threat of all-day rain, and Gordon was glad of it. "Yes," he said and inhaled deeply and exhaled in a noisy way, seeming satisfied, which was how they felt, too. Forgotten were the woozy picnic and the problems of money. After all, Nick and Pie were a handsome couple, young and loved. Aunt Lucinda was rich even if they weren't. Hundreds of people had come to their wedding, and now they were caretakers for a scenic estate called The Cottage. The Cottage on Morgan Bay. For them the sky cleared and the sun came out and the garden began to sizzle. Gordon stayed on. He watched the happy couple, swatted by the waves: how they exhausted themselves until he was exhausted, too, and he slept. They all slept. They slept through the white hours of afternoon when the light was less complex. When they woke, the sand was peachy colored, and the sky was pretty. Gordon said he wanted to do something, but what? Why didn't they have any money!

They had the Crosley. "Fun," Pie said.

"Some fun," Nick said. "You killed some kind of animal in that toy."

Pie said, "I could bike to Gary's and see if he has any clams. We could have a clambake."

"Down here? After five? It's damp and cold and there's not as much beach."

"You come up with something why don't you."

"The lotion's hot. It can't feel good," Gordon said, but Pie said he was wrong.

"I'm so sunburned anything against my skin feels cool," she said.

Gordon wiped his hands on her breasts. He said, "Lovely." He said, "Maybe you'll think of something to do. I'll call you."

A line they had heard before – had used themselves. *I'll call you* augured disappointment.

Nick's handsome face was crinkled. "What the fuck was that all about?"

"What's this?" Pie asked.

"You're more ambitious than I am," was what Nick finally said.

A cup of soup was dinner; the radio, left off.

"Find some music," Pie said and left Nick to wander through The Cottage. She swatted Aunt Lucinda's clothes until she found his idea of ambition: Valentino tap pants, and she tapped downstairs to nobody's music but her quavery own.

"Look at you," he said.

On the beach, they agreed, their daydreaming was sometimes dangerous. The memory of Gordon's misanthropic breath against their faces came in gusts.

"Jesus," Pie said, remembering.

"What?"

The hollows of her body, especially at her hips, were exciting to them both, and they smiled to see the sand running out of Nick's hand and into the ditched place between her hips.

"Jesus," Pie said.

"I was thinking I would lick."

Back to the garden, to the doused and swabbed, every morning, afternoon. Nick staked the droopers and Pie cut back. The heavy-headed mock orange, now past, Pie hacked at and hacked at until the shorn shrub looked embarrassed.

"Poor thing," Nick said.

And Pie laughed. "I've turned the grandpa of the front walk into a kid."

Pie, a long girl, wobbly in heeled shoes, bowlegged, shifty – bored, perhaps – but friendly, quick to laugh, on any errand making an impression. Nick left her on the village green the next afternoon, a lean girl in a ruffled bib. What was she wearing exactly? Something skimpy, faded, pink. She wore braids (again) or that was how Nick remembered her when he described to the police Elizabeth Lathem Day – Pie was her father's invention. A girl, a pretty speck, a part of summer and passing through it.

She was. Pie was a white blond, a blond everywhere – it made Nick hard to think of her. She had close blond fur between her legs. He liked to comb it with his fingers, pull a little bit. Fuck.

"Where the hell is she?" Nick couldn't help himself. "Missing persons – really?"

Lucinda said there was no family precedent; no one was mad that she knew of.

"Don't think we weren't getting along. Quite the opposite."

*   *   *

Dogs off leashes snuffed in the woods. Heavy yellow and black dogs, their rheumy eyes mournful, their hard tails always looked wet and whapped against the shrubs. Once the dogs barked; Nick heard though they were out of sight. They had found something dead and offensive – not her, not Pie – thank God! Although after the dogs, the reports, the calls, the case grew fainter.

Also, also, Nick was drinking. He was forgetting he had this job. He found himself standing in front of open broom closets and cabinets, in front of the dishwasher and sinks. Sometimes his hands were wet.

Watering; he finished watering the wilted patches, then sat on the porch and worried his roughed-up hands, cut and dirty and uncared for, ugly as roots and clumsy. Hard even to phone, to push the buttons accurately, but he did and to his surprise Gordon Brisk answered, and said, "I'm only just home but I've heard. I'm sorry."

And that was that.

What was this guy all about was what Nick wanted to know. "Tell me," Nick said to Lucinda. Addresses, historic districts, the watch he wore, his antique truck, Gordon's conversation was an orange pricked with cloves – an aromatic keepsake of Episcopal Christmases – so it came as a surprise when he said he was a Jew. A Jew?

"You've not seen a lot of the world, Nick."

True, he hadn't. He had married young.

But Nick did not want to travel: he wanted to stay at The Cottage at least until spring, maybe through another summer. Who knew? Pie might come back.

Why would Gordon say more? Nick and Pie hadn't seen him since – when? That hot, flashy day Brisk discovered they only looked rich; they had money enough to get by. But how much was that? How much did it cost to get by pleasantly?

They were young, newly married. The most expensive things they bought were medicinal, recreational.

"You have no idea how happy we have been here," Nick said. This was the truth uttered later, after whatever had passed for dinner, after the bath that made him sweat, the third or fourth Scotch. "We were really, really happy."

The mothers and fathers – on both sides – made visits. They remarked on the garden and the ocean; they said no one would leave such a place voluntarily. So Nick stayed on at The Cottage. He watched the seasons redden then blue then brittle and brown the plants. The decline could be beautiful, but Nick's hands, ungloved, grew grotesque. A fungus buckled and yellowed his thumb-nail. His hands, all rose-nicks and dirt, reminded him of Gordon's hands. Gordon talking about something to do with love, saying they had no idea, speaking in his seer voice, the old, pocked, vacant voice, prophesying horrors they could not imagine.

Not us. Pie thought and Nick thought, too; weren't they always harmonious after Gordon left? They said, "We're lucky." Together: "We are."

"You have no idea," Gordon had said another day on the beach. He had said to Nick, "Someday your mouth will bleed in your sleep, and her cunt, too, will stain whatever it touches."

"Love?"

Gordon in the buff on the beach that time, pulling at the bunched part between his legs, lifting up a purse of excitable skin. The black-haired, peaky creature known as his wife had been a cunt. Gordon had said, "I was on my way home when I saw the smoke. Up in smoke! My wife and some of my paintings." Gordon had asked, "You know what I tried to save, don't you?"

Nick had suspected it was not his wife.

But what was Nick doing to find his?

Why was it Gordon that Nick thought so much about when Gordon had shut up his house and gone somewhere south, southwest?

Oh, the summer! The summer felt next door despite the cold. Nick talked to anybody. He shut the place up. He was there after last call, at the bar, saying his goodbyes at the Clam Box, already shivering yet still polite.

Likable boy.

It was a dry cold, a snowless night, and Nick, so exposed in the Crosley, hurt driving into it. The starless sky was friendly, and the moon, if there was one, was wide.

THE DUCHESS OF ALBANY

"The garden dies with the gardener" was what Owen had said, but when, years later, he died, she faced the garden with a will to keep it alive – as who would not? But the twins urged her to sell. They thought it would be wise to move out of the house (for too long too large) and into Wax Hill with its assisted care conveniences and attached hospital: Wax Hill that short line to the furnace and the thoroughfare. She had carried Owen's chalky bones in a bag. She had tossed him into every part of the garden. How could she sell the house when from every window in the house – and there were lots of windows – she could see some part of him, Owen, her well-named spirit with meaty gardener's hands and other contradictions. He liked the slow and melancholy; he listened to Saint Matthew's Passion long after Easter. But God? He didn't believe. Young once, he saw himself alone when he was old with just a daughter. He left behind two, not of his own making but full of reverence for him, nonetheless. He was a schoolteacher and the luggage-colored oak leaves signaled his season, but it had come around so fast. He had had nuns for cousins – nuns! Sisters of Charity, how queer they seemed now; their menace, vanished. Mustachioed Agnes Gertrude and arthritic Mary Agnes, they had taught at the Mount for forty-odd years, wimpled and sudden, full of authority. She said, "I haven't seen a nun in such a long, long time."

The twins, on conference call, were hard to tell apart except when they laughed. She didn't have a lot to say and lapsed into what the weather was doing.

Today snow, the second snowstorm of the new year – and Owen once in it. She could see him, lopsided, clowny, a scarf around his head. Blizzardy weather was wonderful to walk in.

"Oh, Mother," from the twins when she cried. Overly dramatic. Yes, she knew she was being, but she missed him. The wide road he had offered her each morning, saying, "What's on your agenda?" Now that wide road had all the charm of a freeway.

"Take a walk," the twins said, "if it's snowing."

Inward would be a nice word for what she was, self-absorbed would be more accurate.

"I know the country is at war," she said; nevertheless, she missed him. "Besides, when I look at the larger world, I cry almost as much."

But Owen, his voice, the sound of him in another room. Off-key hummer, cracking nuts over the paper, singing or whistling a patter song. A Gilbert and Sullivan tune twiddled for days: "The lady novelist . . . she surely won't be missed." Whatever he thought to play or heard was his favorite G and S. "I've got a little list . . . she surely won't be missed."

Some nights now she plunged into working, but some mornings vodka was preferred. She had to admit it – to herself but not to the twins.

She told them, "I have started a sestina." She said she was inspired by Elizabeth Bishop's sestina, and she was using two of the same words. "'Time to plant tears,' was what moved me."

"Sestinas are difficult," the twins said. Her educated daughters, they knew, they had tried. "In high school, Mother. Remember Miss Byrd?"

"Oh, Miss Byrd!" And they had a rare good laugh, the three of them, she and the twins, remembering the ethereal teacher, giddy and overworked and walking into walls. The twins laughed about Miss Byrd getting lost in the mall on the Boston trip. The twins were laughing and she was laughing a little, too, when the sight of the old dog asleep alarmed her. And all of a sudden, in the whiplash moodiness of bygone youth, she was mad at Owen. Damn him. "There's no pleasure to be had in discipline and restraint," she said to the twins; "that's what a fucking sestina is all about," and so the pleasure of laughing was over.

"Why, Mother?" one voice.

The other said, "You've been drinking."

She said, "I don't have to defend myself." Besides, she explained the drinking was a problem only if she drove, "and I don't." She stayed at the table or slept in the big chair and no one need worry. She might die there – no mess.

"Mother!"

"All I am saying is you can't have much of an accident if you sit somewhere with a drink."

"You have to get up for the bottle." Only Clarissa would say that. Here was the difference between her girls: one was meaner than the other.

"I bring the bottle to the table."

"Great, Mother. That's just great. Now do you see why we don't want to call?"

"Then don't. Leave me alone." And she hung up the phone and almost kicked at the dog, but she refrained. The dog was her friend. Owen's dog, Pink. "Poor old Pink," she said, "you scared the shit out of me," and she leaned out to pat a shapeless pile of fuzz and spoke nonsense to it. Pink, adopted, a miniature mix of something abandoned and abused. Pink was hairless at the start. "Look at you now, you little dustcloth, baby Pink, old sweetie. I wouldn't hurt you. You're my pal."

"I'm on the move today," she said, but the dog lay unperturbed, sure she would come back.

A snowstorm, a thaw, a brilliant sun, snow, freez-ing temperatures, snow, then better, warmer, prom-ising weather arrived, and she looked back at Pink and then to the rake and the garden where the wet, mahogany islands of leaves, submerged for months in snow, now floated. All the snow pelted away by a rain the night before and only a mist this morning, something more than fog. She liked to work in it. She thought of Owen's hair – water-beaded and in the sun brightly netted. She raked and thought if only the twins could see. If they could live with the garden the way she did. Covered or uncovered, leafed or bare, the garden was restorative in any season. The persistent mist was turning into rain. March, late March. Somebody's birthday – whose?

She abandoned Pink to the mud. She raked the beds; she swept the pavers. "Dirty girl!" she said when the dog wobbled toward her. Why had she even taken the poor mutt out? The dog trembled and squeaked.

The six words in her sestina are: garden, widow, hus-band, dog, almanac, tears. "The envoy is an oncoming train." She said, "Restrain the wild element of mourning or what you get is sentimentality."

The twins, she should listen to them, sell, move, secure what there was to secure for them. Poor girls, in the disarray of single life, the yap, yap, yap of the dryer at the laundromat beating up their tired clothes.

Few single men where they lived, and the best of them gay.

The rain was cold but she let herself get wet the way Owen did until she was soaked.

In the kitchen again she lit up the stove and watched the rain wash the garden into its outline. Green spikes stippled the beds she had raked, and the cropped crowns of established plants, the wheat-colored stalks of hydrangea, poked out polished in a design of circles mostly. If her daughters could only see.

How is it possible that in caring for the garden she could miss summer? How is it possible, but she did.

Up at four and again at five, and at five-thirty up for good. Pink was awake; she heard the dog tick against the bare floor, circling the bed. "Good morning," she said, and she went on talking to Pink as she carried the dog down the stairs and to the paper. "Because it's too cold outside, isn't it, Pinkie? I'm not going to do what I did yesterday. Too cold and wet this morning." She saw forty-five on the thermometer. The radio said it was colder. She got water, aspirin, more water. She put on deodorant, then went back to bed. For how long? Who cared? She was up again besides. She washed her hair and dried it in the heat of the open oven.

Once she had thought it would be hard to let go of life, but it will not be so hard.

She read; she wrote; she must have had lunch but

she could not remember. The scenes that blew past came out in bands of color. The wispy complication of bare branches was added magic; the shadows were dark and sure. She put Owen in her poem, Owen or the shape of him, on the deck in his coat and pom-pom hat, a passenger on a steamer, a blanket over his legs, heavy sweater, scarf – the silly hat. The garden beyond him she turned into straw.

Why did she lie to the twins? Why, when they called, did she say, "I am not drinking. I am working"? Why didn't she tell them, "I'm doing both"? The brief hello of summer and its long, long goodbye. Great piles of death she hauled to the woods to the deadpile and tossed. Farewell to the flowers of summer, plume poppy and vernonia. Turk's-cap lilies, delicate as paper lanterns at the height of their glowing, goodbye.

"Anytime you care to look," Owen said, whenever he caught her watching his quick strip at the back door. She liked to look at his secreted machinery from behind when he bent over or stood one-legged getting out of his shorts. There it was, the long, dark purse of him asway. The head of his cock was the color of putty. Its expression was aloof most of the time, a self-satisfied indifference. When he was seated in some other ablution, the head of his cock was rosy and large and also arousing. All she ever had to do was ask when what she liked to do was look.

Look!

"It's yours," he said, and with a flourish held out the bouquet of himself; "be my guest."

Overnight, age seemed to happen to him, then a few years of *ifs*, poorer health, medication.

"Don't talk of moving just yet, please," she told the twins. "Not tonight." Why, except for loneliness, did she answer the phone? (Owen at the long table, saying to the ringing phone, "Go away, people. Leave us alone," and people pretty much did.) To get off the phone she used the excuse of Pink somewhere sick. The odd thing was when she did hang up, she found Pink in the closet, sick.

"Poor baby," she said.

"Old age," said the vet.

He gave Pink pills that worked to ward off motion sickness which sometimes happened to old pets, despite their stationary lives. "She will sleep a little bit more."

"A good night's sleep," she said. "Wouldn't that be nice?"

They talked a little, she and the old vet, for he, too, was old. They talked about Owen, or she did, and he asked, "Have you looked for any groups?" On the drive home in the rain, she cried and she couldn't see to drive and had to pull over. "Fucking old vet!" She put her face in her hands and cried. She petted Pink and cooed, saying, "We won't go back there again, will we, Pinkie? No, no. But you feel better already, don't you?" The little dog was a dust ball; just petting Pink made her feel awful. "Do I have to outlive everybody?"

"Yes, yes, yes, no," she said. "The lily of the valley is up." She said, "Yes, it was two years ago today."

"We wanted you to know, we're thinking about you," the twins said, and the girls called again later just to see how she was. "How are you, Mommy?" they asked in maternal voices.

"The lily of the valley is up," she said.

May, his birthday month and hers, when she and Owen quietly celebrated with nothing more than mild surprise. He was given to saying, "I think I'm going to see another spring," And he did — just.

Heart.

Of course, his heart, what else?

Now the oppressive immovable quality of objects wore her out.

"Mother!"

Whatever was not in front of her she meant to remember. His shapely head, his small red ears, his hair.

"You've been drinking. We can tell."

"We knew you would."

"So why act so surprised?" She hung up the phone and saw the fucking dog peeing on the floor in front of her. Little fucker!

They had not had enough time, she and Owen.

"I'm no such thing," she said to the twins.

Another night, "I'm tired."

Another, "I'm old is what it is."

Owen had said that in the garden she would rediscover childhood, but those childhood experiences she remembered were mostly dreadful. She took her nose out of the flower, and her cousin, seeing her, laughed. "Your nose!" The red was hard to get off as were grass stains on her knees and elbows. Childhood in the garden. The garden was not genteel. The garden was full of thugs, and Owen had shown her some. The Duchess of Albany was not a thug, but a racer on a brittle stem, a clematis with deep pink upside-down bells, deceptively frail and well-bred, small, timorous bells. The Duchess of Albany was a favorite of hers: how could she sell the house to someone who might kill the Duchess in the earthmoving business of house improvement?

"The men came, yes," she said to her daughters. "But they have such big feet!" she said. "They can't help it, I know."

"Mommy!" the twins said. "We're only trying to help."

So was she. Hadn't she consented to the ugly tub? That ugly tub with the roughed bottom and the grips.

Her children have not visited in years.

"Oh, Mother," they say, "what are you talking about?"

She took her own safety precautions and moved her bedroom, such as it was, downstairs to the sunporch. On the sunporch in the sofa she was not afraid to fall asleep.

What made Pink nest in corners? "What do you think is the matter?" she asked.

"Pink's old, Mommy."

"The dog's ancient. Take her to the vet."

"Oh, God," she said. Going to the old vet frightened her as much as it did the dog. "Oh, God," she said. She felt so bogged down and muddled.

"You're drunk is what you are": from the meanest?

"Oh God," she said. "I don't want to find a stiff dog under the desk. I don't, I don't, I don't." She cried and the twins consoled her.

"Mommy, why don't you crawl into your cream puff and go to sleep for a while?"

"You and the dog have a snooze."

She said, "I think I will." She said, "Pink doesn't realize I have mixed feelings about her."

She had found him in an odd posture tipped against the shed. The hose was squiggled over half the garden, and elsewhere were two full buckets, a shovel, a rake.

How she had wished, for his sake, Owen had put away the tools and coiled the hose and achieved a perfect death although the twins yelled at her for saying such a thing.

But the morning after he died, the terrible morning after, repeats so many times a day: she woke up, dressed, walked downstairs, made her gritty breakfast drink, and took her tea outside. Then she saw it, the grain bin, where he kept his garden clothes, and she fell to her knees and cried. Up to that moment, she had sipped at her tea and believed he was alive and already in the garden and muddy.

The permanence of his absence is a noise she hears when she listens to how quiet. How he did and he did and he did for her.

"Can I be of any help?" Always he asked this, "Do you want anything? Can I get you anything?"

She thought it was summer still if not spring but the day's evidence said it was fall. Again!

"When was the last time you were outside, Mommy?"

"I'm taking care of the garden." She told them her nose was in it, brushing against the staining anthers, freakishly marked, a bald animal, she, a stiff, kinked dog, not unlike the dog she owned. Pink. Pink, what was the matter with that dog? After she got off the phone, she caught her in the act and pulled her away, made her stop, put Pink out of doors – like that – then wiped up after her. She brought Pink inside and carried Pink to her bed in the kitchen and talked to her. But even as she apologized for the choke hold, a part of her wished Pink dead and another part feared her dying, and she took Pink upstairs and bathed her in the new tub. Her pink skin was so pink she looked scalded. She was thin; Pink shivered though she was gentle and the water was warm. She dried Pink with her own soft towel and when the dog was dried and happy and at ease, she swaddled and rocked Pink. She was so pitifully thin. She put the little dog in her cream puff and said, "I'm getting into mine."

FAMILY MAN

Tonight, on the shore of a low lake in a low spot in the Kettle Moraine – black water, churchy trees – Maas sees his concave wife in urgent conversation with their daughter Grace. Sly girl, long hair slung over one shoulder, bare ear cocked close to whatever her mother is saying to her, Grace, all of a sudden, turns on her heel to see him looking at her. Then Grace is standing next to him. With the slightest attention, he has charmed her away from the conversation she was having with his wife, her mother, to walk with him. She talks in a small voice without showing her teeth. Maas moves closer to hear. It may be the way she uses her tight lips, but he can't hear her and bends close to ask has she ever been in love, when his wife rushes up from behind.

So Maas leaves the women and turns back to the house.

The next morning, he bolts a split birch trunk together and it bleeds.

*   *   *

Theirs, a country-quiet life, is satisfying or should be. His daughter hoped something would happen and it did in the shape of a man blued by symbols that crinkled when he tensed his arms. Maas watched shapes rustle on the man and saw, too, that his wrist was wreathed – royal; and he was not young; he was ready to inherit.

Opalesce is a gauzy word to describe what the sky is doing. From the picture window Maas follows winter colors: whites, slates, steely skies, and yellows. He puts his hand out to the show and feels the cool glass against his palm and is steadied by the sensation. His lovely boxed life: snow falling outside, very pretty, while he stands inside, well and warm, entirely comfortable in comfortable shoes. The past sleds behind him. Door County, 1951: poking raw squirrel over smoky coals, washing the meal down with whiskey. Scant comforts. Even indoors the scratchy camp blankets felt wet. He was most often cold. Early morning whooping into Lake Michigan then gibbering back to a tasteless breakfast of something gluey they ate with a spoon. No cream to cut his coffee. No cushions for the austere chairs on which they sat, Maas, butt-numbed and dumb. 1951. The year he met his wife.

He hears his name, but has no desire to know how he might be described in the future: a glass of water, a flavorless man, at best, at best, on a white tablecloth a goblet of melted ice with the slightest curl of lemon in it. Through the blinds a blade of sunlight cuts the glass in half and shows up dust.

WHERE YOU LIVE?
WHEN YOU NEED ME?

Out of nowhere, Ella, a mound with no known address, a swaying mystery, swollen hands, swollen feet – did she sleep in the playground? Ella simply appeared. No phone, but a tiny notepad, a tiny pencil: *Where you live? When you need me?* Like the Mister Softee sound, Ella drew children to her under the shawl of her arms. Ella was a house in the park for an afternoon, an afternoon that often faded into later – *No trouble. Anytime. Where you live? When you need me?* She wasn't a bargain, but she was worth every penny. Besides, Anne Byrnne, who first used Ella, said the woman spent her money on treats for the children. How else to explain the Matchbox trucks I found in my sons' pockets?

Uh, Ella?

I like it, they're happy.

Me too, but you need the money!

That was the summer when little parts of little bodies turned up in KFC buckets in Dumpsters in the city, the summer of 1984, weeks of record heat and brown air. Colonies of plague-ugly rats partied under park benches, hauling off big finds, pretzels and buns, acting bold. Ella watched the children by the playground sprinklers, then picnicked in the park when the sun was down and the grass blue, the rats less visible. I saw Ella sometimes in the north meadow, a squat teepee, circled by the Byrnne boys chasing the little Flemming girl with squirt guns, getting sopped. For a while we fretted over losing Ella to the Flemmings. Everyone shared Ella. She had work every day if she wanted. *No,* Ella said, *I don't leave,* then agreed to two weeks in July with the Flemmings in Nantucket even though by her own admission she couldn't swim.

Ella brought out something in the mothers I knew, brought out something in me, so that I, we, all of us recklessly employed someone about whom we knew next to nothing in a summer when the streets at night looked greasy and baby body parts were being found. No one who hired Ella that summer ever knew with any certainty her last name, let alone her address – even the efficient Anne Byrnne was unsure. Ella asked to be paid in cash.

Anne Byrnne probably did know Ella's last name, but she was gutting an apartment on Fifth – taking out walls, putting in new windows – and she was living in the apartment at the same time with two boys, five and twoish, which, when I think about it now, was clearly unsafe. The barricades were useless; the boys ducked under. I see her younger son now toddling toward an open window.

What a summer. A third and last reported bucket was found downtown, off Bowery. As with the other bodies, the head was gone. Oddly, no report of a missing baby was ever made in any borough. Maybe the children were from out of state?

I came home later than planned one night and found Ella sitting in the summer dark, which was not so dark I couldn't see her, but I wondered why not a light was on. She sat monumentally boulder-like, but alive, hands as big as soup bowls stacked in her lap.

Something else. At the end of the season I stood on a slimy ledge of a waterfall with my younger son when he stepped out and I grabbed his bib overalls just in time. What were we standing on? Why were we there? We were in the Berkshires renting a house on a small muddy lake is all I remember. That and the sound of water and its tinkly music over and over.

I believed in God back then, too. And nobody knows where he comes from.

BURST PODS, GONE-BY, TANGLED ASTER

Young as they appear to be, the house painters have daughters old enough to complain about, which they do, to each other, across an expanse of a few feet on ladders at the south-facing second-story windows of the house.

From the start, Peg has stayed in the house and watched from different windows as the boys have painted. She just hopes Pat Farkey keeps sending these boys.

She can barely say hello to the house painters, so abashed is she by their hearty sweetness and the lives she imagines for them.

Peg talks to the kitchen chairs. She's doped, of course, but the furniture is company. The young house painters lean against their truck and smoke. Smoking . . . she did that once.

Her husband Anders watches the boys smoke, says something, makes them smile, or are they grimacing a little? Has he cornered them or asked something off-color, personal – *You getting any?* That sort of thing. She's heard his coarse approximations of street talk, young talk. She's heard him asking girls, *Now who's your boyfriend?* then lapping up their shy response.

Anders did the Rite Aid business today and – no surprise – got to talking with the pharmacist Stephanie. He likes Stephanie. "Girl's open as a penny," he says. True. But Peg can hardly face her.

Stephanie was the one to fill their daughter's last newest failed prescription, the inflating and idiot-making pills that turned the girl into a parade balloon in need of handlers – chiefly her mother – the ones that made her quiet, helped her sleep, helped her wake, once a day, twice a day, twice a day with meals. Who doses her at Medfield? Peg doesn't know. They're not allowed to see her: the doctors think it best.

There's nothing much to talk about over lunch but Pat Farkey's painters, and yes, as far as Anders is concerned, they are the best on the peninsula, yes, he is happy with the job so far.

Anders catches the door before it slams and it seems he might say more but what she halfway hears is Anders calling Ridge or Rodge? Redge? What is it? She looks out the window over the sink and sees that Ridge is the one in a pirate scarf in a squat painting the railing. Okay. And hearing Anders, the boy springs up on ropy haunches, nods in greeting. She turns a knife in her hands and looks hard at this Ridge and then through the boy to the woods again and their neighbor's field of brown stalks and burst pods, gone-by, tangled aster. She thumbs the blade, then uses the knife to skin the watery scum off the blackened breadboard, scrapes strings and stems into the compost bag and potato peels from dinner's burger pie – my God, they do go on eating and eating. Maybe she's pushing for earlier meals to make the days pass faster.

Your disappointments are mine: she had said this to Andie, to her daughter, Andie, in her boneless body – short neck, soft chin, smally featured moon face. What was a mother to make of such a face really? Say, *It's much like mine?*

Peg knew the horrors of undressing, the crimped grooves of waistbands and camel-toed panties. A boy in school told Andie she looked like a muffin top, which Andie took at first to mean a good thing until her brother Carl told her, "It's your gut hanging over your jeans." What was the matter with him? Hurts, prickly, hive-like bites, little poisons Peg can't scratch out: "Maybe it's the moles on your face that make you look old, Mom" – and the boy had said worse, but she didn't always remember.

"They call Andie a gunt," he'd said.

She doesn't want to remember *gunt* but the hamburger grays in the pan; and the memory of gut, cunt, gunt, and Carl's mouth, new beard, raw skin is upended by Carl himself loudly arrived — *Hi, Mom* — and behind him, his girlfriend Lee-Ann, both smiling as if they like her, as if they come by every day and are expected.

"Dad invited us."

"He didn't tell me."

Anders points out the brushwork on the porch rail's skinny spindles. "Come out and look!" The name Farkey is on his lips though it's that kid, Ridge, the house painter, who's done the work Anders praises. Peg watches Carl and Anders and Lee-Ann as they look up at the spindles and the scrolled eaves on the house, this old farmhouse, once, a hundred years ago, a teahouse for the quarry down the road. A plaque near the front door reads: Fern Cottage 1888. The name is Anders's invention, a dainty tea-like name and a nod to the ostrich ferns that thrive in the dark borders of the lower garden.

What is Anders saying to these unexpected guests — so that now Peg has to double up on potatoes and cut limp carrots for a side dish to a stretched-thin dinner of gray burger pie. The business makes her angry, even as she puts out unsalted saltines and low-fat cheese, and when Lee-Ann reaches out her loose inky arms, Peg sees smeary numbers and a wreath tattoo. She doesn't want to know what the tattoo stands for, doesn't want to know much at all, it seems.

Now, for instance, Carl is talking about auto body parts online – alternators or motor mounts, belts. Something he can get cheap.

"I want a Jaguar," Lee-Ann says.

"Hunh."

Carl, who has been listening for anything Lee-Ann might say, takes up with Anders again about a Corvette he could fix if only . . .

"If Dad lends you money?"

"No, Mom."

"Fixing cars," she says, "costs money."

"I'm talking about Hardy's car."

"I said, fixing cars . . ."

"You deaf? I'm talking about Hardy's car. What he needs to fix it. I could fix it. I could make some money fixing it, Peg."

"Don't call me Peg."

"Well, whoever you are, everything doesn't have to do with money."

"I'm not saying."

"That's all you've said, all you ever say is how much, how much. How much the painting's costing and how Farkey's never here but lets his kids do the work. Kids younger than me. I should be doing the painting, right?"

"Nothing to fight about now," Anders says.

She says, "I like the house painters. They have children. They're married."

"Yeah, real grown-up, I bet, and living happily ever blah, blah."

"You want to pick a fight, Carl?"

"Peg, please."

"This is why I hate coming here," Carl pushes away from the table and Peg makes for the boy, grabs at his shirt.

"Don't you think you're a little old for a teenager, Carl?"

Lee-Ann, the teenager, looks to what Carl does and follows him out, saying nothing as Carl talks loudly about Peg, the bitch. Is it any wonder Dad wants company?

Carl turned thirty-seven last March very quietly at the kitchen table over double-trouble chocolate cupcakes Peg has made for him for almost as many years. The girlfriend was missing, but Carl had seemed happy to Peg then, maybe not to her husband, Anders, no; maybe not as happy as the house painters, but celebrating in a house with a ghost for company, what could they expect?

Not much. He has an apartment. Anders helps with the rent because Carl's only part-time at the dry cleaner. He's otherwise, or says he is otherwise, taking mechanic courses at Ramapo. His nights, his days, his progress in the tech course, she doesn't ask, Carl doesn't report.

Peg makes the double-trouble cupcakes for herself as much as for him. A bowl-licker, a spatula-sucker, she doesn't stint on sugar and it shows, even though the boy ate most of them. She hasn't beaten the eat-healthy drum very loudly, doesn't mention weight. Sleeveless dresses still chafe her arms, and underpants yank up her crack and hurt so that she stands still or moves hardly at all.

One year, the boy wanted cherry pie à la mode, and Peg made both, the pie and the double-trouble cupcakes.

Today she is barefoot in what Anders calls her farmer pants, bib overalls, softly comfortable, but loose as an old slipcover, and she is saddened to think she looks like a sofa, except that now she has no daughter to complain about – once, but no more.

Every time Peg looks at her right hand, she sees another kinked or swollen part visit her.

THE DOT SISTERS

In the windy city they sway on a bridge and let the wind get under their dresses, Claire and Julia, happy. Let them be happy. They have suffered. Their father abandoned them years ago; their mother rages past, shrill ghost. Swipe her away; stay with the girls on the bridge in the high wind in the summer of 1970. How cheerful they appear against the passing scene in navy, gray, or khaki. The sisters wear matching dot dresses, green ground for Claire; for Julia, brown. The river beneath them is tan, not brown, and the sky overhead is true blue. Probably they have been happy together before, but Julia is often melancholy and Claire is pessimistic, so it has been a long time since – *or never!*

Never?

Don't be ridiculous, Julia says. They are simply happier than they have been in a long, long time. They've sold the house; the estate is settled. They think they will not come back.

They should pack tonight, take the train tomorrow.

Christine Schutt

The Palmetto sounds breezy. Travel to the Carolinas to a tall white inn, tippy as a cake with balconies, shutters, netting, and flutter, where crystal chandeliers bejewel every room and on the bedside table a swan carafe of water; on the pillow, chocolates in foil. Let them be comforted. Please. Let them sleep. Not in every dream, unpacked, undressed, shamed. Enough with the nakedness and shit and sick pets sick in corners.

Mrs. Pall-Meyer, short-waisted, stooped, breasts shrunk to teardrops, Mrs. Pall-Meyer was a dirty old woman, no matter she was rich. What good had money done her? She was traveling alone. They were both, Arden Fawn and Mrs. Pall-Meyer, traveling alone, but Mrs. Pall-Meyer had been at the ranch for over a month and would ride on long after Arden went home: Monday, next week, the first of April, home to an airbrushed county Arden once thought harmless.

Arden yanked at her reins and brought Doc into line while the old woman, Mrs. Pall-Meyer, held back her horse and put even more space between them. Mrs. Pall-Meyer was as friendless as Arden; no one would miss them.

They rode to the dried-out creek bed that devolved to a trail of ashy sand, charred wood, and trash not pictured in the ranch brochure – a strip of fender, a Pringles can – the rubbly blight of modern life, no green in sight but dust. At least for a time the sound of the horses was peaceable, but the hard floor of the desert came on with a clap. A wizened spring, the sickly prickly pear and organ pipe cacti were so riddled with holes they might have been targets. Even the paloverde trees looked leached. They rode along a level path, fording dried-out riverbeds of chalky stones – pale landscape, white sun. She put on her sunglasses and the view, honeyed, was not so hard on the spirit, but her back still hurt; it felt as if she were tightening a belt of barbed wire around her waist – God almighty, it hurt, and the ride had hardly begun. Arden rode apart not so much by choice as that it happened. Terrain had nothing to do with it. Her horse was slow and she was heavy.

Mrs. Pall-Meyer, even farther behind, was a stick and rode as she liked. Now she went at a gentle pace and comfortable distance, for which Arden was grateful. In this way, far enough apart from all of the others, Arden could play on in her pioneering dream of self-sufficiency, even though her favorite part of the ride was when she was off the horse and walking to the ranch. Her legs felt used and wide apart then, and her walk was more a straddle.

"Kick him!" Mrs. Pall-Meyer cried. The old woman threatened to pass. They had fallen too far behind.

Arden's horse started to lope then lapsed into a rough trot stopped by the earthy rump of the dentist's enormous horse.

"Oh, hoh, my," Arden moaned. Knocked against the saddle horn, her pubic bone stung and she pressed her hand between her legs: she felt her own heat and heard Mrs. Pall-Meyer spit. Mrs. Pall-Meyer had paused, as had all the riders, at the incline.

"How long have you been riding?" Mrs. Pall-Meyer asked.

"Oh," Arden, said, shifting in the saddle, "all my life, but not a lot."

Mrs. Pall-Meyer, the name suggesting a hyphenated importance, merely snorted and rode ahead.

The trail turned narrower, rougher, stonier although the redheaded wrangler – Red, for his hair – might have been asleep, so little did the ride's danger impress him. How many times had he led folks up this route?

"Over five thousand acres gives a guy a lot of different ways to go," he answered. "You'd be surprised."

Mrs. Pall-Meyer said, "If I had something to ride on." In this way, she simply went on talking to herself, making tough, irritated pickax sounds with words like crap, drink, think. For all the advantages she must have had, Mrs. Pall-Meyer was a coarse woman. She had made herself known in the morning, talking at the young Asbach boy, Ben, "My friends are dead. My sister is demented. I'm the last of my line, but I bet you've got a lot of friends." Oh, the nuisance of them all was what the old woman meant to say in her supercilious voice.

Arden had looked on at how Mrs. Pall-Meyer befuddled the boy and made him blush. Ben Asbach of the Asbachs – "There are eight of us here," said the matriarch merrily. A granddaughter – slight as straw – called Mrs. Asbach Nana.

What names, if any, had others at the ranch assigned her? – Arden, Arden Fawn. Was she the fat lady, the dull lady, the shy lady – hair color as uncertain as her age? Arden had a pretty face, of this much she was certain, which made it all the sadder, the weight. She hoped for her horse's sake she would soon reach the summit.

There, Red said they could get off their horses and stretch their legs. But Arden had no intention of stretching her legs. If she got off her horse, she would never get on again. Besides, she could see just as well from on top of her horse, and her back wouldn't hurt if Doc held still. The riding itself, walking, walking especially and however precariously, was easiest on her back. No loping, please! They rode up the mountain, slowly and close, and her thoughts were the same and body-centered until they all stopped at the summit. The sturdy banker loudly huffed off his horse and landed hard; his wife tiptoed lightly – all grace. And Arden?

"You sure?" Red asked, ready to help.

"I'm fine," she said. "No, I'll stay on."

118

So Red adjusted her saddle, pulled it more to his side, asked after Doc.

"He's a good boy," Arden said and wondered was Red a good boy or did he fuck sheep? Arden liked to appall herself with her own appalling thoughts. She liked a little fright in the middle of small exchanges – the self-manufactured fright from thinking she was overheard. The dentist's wife, who rode near and behind Red, asked him about the drought with an informed interest in its effects on the region's wildlife.

Arden regarded the dentist's wife, talking about water tables. Maybe in some states this was called flirting but the pity of it: a late-life romance as brief as a paper match, a piff of heat but no flame really, a glow quickly extinguished.

The dentist himself winked at Arden. "Not going to get off and stretch your legs?" he asked.

"Never. I couldn't. How would I get on again?"

The dentist, smiling, said, "There's lots of ways."

The dentist was a small man darkly outlined by his specialty, a dentist for expensive and serious procedures to do with reconstruction – think of the bright pan with its sharp slender instruments – she did and was afraid of what this dentist would do inside her mouth. His jeans looked new and his shirt was very white, unwrinkled, snap-buttons, western. She watched him move to a higher point and a different perspective.

Oh, hell, strike the match of romance, who cares if it's short? Why else had she come to the Double-D? Should she say the weather, the birdlife, the desert in bloom? No one had mentioned a drought. Scant birdlife this season, no color, but hovering just behind Arden was Mrs. Pall-Meyer. Mrs. Pall-Meyer, an imperious crone with a pointy face that jabbed, Mrs. Pall-Meyer stood for something, but for what? Oh, the obvious, death or the future.

There, leaning against a rock and eating ranch granola was the little Asbach girl, rapt with her story's unspooling. Her lips moved and she smiled to herself, frowned, pouted, then smiled again. Arden guessed she was ten or eleven, a cozy year, fifth grade, but what was her story about? What could she be saying?

Movement now. The others in the group were getting on their horses again. Only Mrs. Pall-Meyer did not. She was protesting about her horse.

"Want some help?" Red asked.

"What do you think?" Mrs. Pall-Meyer, with one foot in Red's hands, said, "I hate having to ride a dull horse." She tipped a little trying to look at Red as she talked, unsteady, so that he lifted her until she swung her crooked body over the beast she dismissed as a plodder. She didn't say thank you, just tocked in the saddle to make herself comfortable. It occurred to Arden that Mrs. Pall-Meyer might be drunk.

Red took the lead and the party stayed together, the horses picked their way, butt-close, along a ledge. Steep, narrow, white, the ledge was dramatic and Arden held her breath. No one spoke; quiet but for the clocking noise of the horses, their gassy sighs and shivers. Stones popped and the trail noise sounded serious – just as in the cowboy movies: after the shoot-out comes the slow descent, hints of danger and exhaustion. The palomino stumbled and some of the ledge fell away.

"We are going down, aren't we?" Arden asked, anxious.

Mrs. Pall-Meyer snorted.

Okay, the question was stupid but the riding was more rocking from side to side than moving forward. *Lean back* had been the instruction for going downhill, and dutifully Arden did – had – even though the small of her back ached and she was afraid of her horse.

The old woman, suddenly seeming close, sneered, "He knows what he's doing."

"I hope so."

"You've really no business on this ride."

"I don't," Arden said. "I don't know," she began but she didn't want to turn around to address the old woman, riding last again. She was tearful enough as it was – her back ached – and to see Mrs. Pall-Meyer's disdain would surely make her cry. She said no more and the repetitive sound of striking hooves stupefied her and when she woke the trail had begun to level off to a more inviting path, soft, quiet, broad. She kicked Doc into a bumpy trot that didn't last long though it put more space between her and Mrs. Pall-Meyer, Mrs. Pall-Meyer now far behind until Red shouted out: "Mrs. Pall-Meyer!"

Why did he?

But Mrs. Pall-Meyer didn't respond.

"What can I . . ." from Red, inconclusive, and so through fluff adrift they rode in a meditative quiet. The banker had spread his life around miles ago. And Red wasn't much of a talker. Now the stables were in sight. There was the pasture where the ranch horses socialized; there, the barn, the tack room, the ring. The ranch, on a hill, Arden couldn't see any part of, but the corral was miraculously close.

She barely heard Red say "Shit!" before he jerked his horse around and rode full out to where Mrs. Pall-Meyer was turned upside down. Her foot, twisted, was caught in the stirrup; most of her lay on the ground. Her horse stood still, unmoved by crisis. What sound was this that Mrs. Pall-Meyer was making, but it was familiar.

A small truck, its trunk down, banged alongside the fence, stopped at the gate, and another wrangler from another direction came out to herd Arden's group into the corral. The banker frisked home, and the dentist's wife and the dentist followed. The Asbachs, grandmother and granddaughter, were already dismounting. "Don't look," the grandmother was saying. Arden saw the fluid ten-year shape slide off her horse and canter on her own once her boots hit the ground. Turn away, little girl, turn away from the future, and she did.

THE LADY FROM CONNECTICUT

Nearly alone on the station platform, she is a heavy, heaving woman, encircled with luxe bags that scuff the pavement when she leans over and sighs. The reassuring blood rush to the head says she's alive with the body's store of surprises, the tics and pricks and stars bright as foil when she opens her eyes. Shadow movement in the parking lot, nothing more, a quiet beseeming a bedroom suburb. She pokes at her phone to call home, seeing not numbers so much as the all-purpose islanded kitchen, her own, something more than a kitchen: polished granite surfaces in speckled pheasant colors. Everything put away and out of sight. Clean, clean. A built-in table and banquette – slide in, slide over, but no one is at the table or in the kitchen. Muted news flickers on the flat screen: gaudy mayhem.

The phone ceases to ring and she hears her bullshit message – the twinkly *Thanks so much for calling!*

"Hey," she says now. "It's me." She sways. "I thought you'd be here. I'm in Dart, a little tipsy." She hears herself wheeze, and they must hear, too, if they hear her at all.

Earlier tonight her friend had said, "Sweets. We're lucky. We've money in our pockets, and the night is not at all cold but clear, fall, and fragrant!"

Ah, who wouldn't love her friend?

"I should have married you, Bebe!" she had said, and not for the first time.

"Shoulda, coulda," was her answer – Bebe, happily divorced and in love with a younger woman.

Why wait at Dart station? Why wait in the Plexiglas shed? Why sit on a cold metal seat with holes she can feel the cold through?

Attend, and so she does and walks away from the station and toward town. She walks steadily enough, follows the yellow flares of the street trees in street light, walks on what she perceives as the upright side of the commercial street, past the jewelry store still golden despite the empty cases; past the rustic café with its washed floors and upended stools, past the gift store and the dry cleaner's scrolled script – *Trafalgar's* – white walls, white counter dramatically backdropped by a heavy black curtain behind which hang bagged clothes. The ceiling light is a chandelier. Who said Dart was dangerous?

Between buildings in the back: a parking lot, plank fence, hedge, sometimes a Dumpster but the lots look swept. Commerce ceases, the sidewalk narrows, and leaf-fall, stomped to leaf-meal, dusts her shoes.

An old sidewalk buckled and cracked in places; houses set back behind leathery rhododendrons – sullen and thuggish. She hates rhododendrons. Big-deal ugly cerise blossoms, they belong in the forest, not ringed around a house.

Her hands are hot and hurt; the handles of the luxe bags cut into them.

Carry on!

She is fifty-six but strong, and ahead at the turn is Saint Francis Church, the turn she takes when she drives to the station, but car conflicts meant the party planner for Big D's upcoming birthday drove her to the station this morning. She has not employed this planner before but has wandered through his parties, admiring his use of bent forks and burlap amid flats of fragile, fringy plants.

But the flowers are the least of preparing for Big D's party. The guests, the seating. Where to put Big D's noisy nephew, a pontificating vegetarian who makes everyone uncomfortable about food?

Set down your burden, Saint Francis says, and so she does: she sets aside her luxe bags and rubs her sore hands. She sits on a bench in front of the church, satchel in lap, there to contemplate the tonsured saint, arms beseeching, palms upturned. But such shallow – shallow hands! What could he hold out to anyone or could anyone take hold of? Saint Francis of Assisi should have birds about his person, shouldn't he? A rabbit somewhere, a squirrel, a fox?

She misses having a dog, sweet Lucy, misses her son – misses his younger self who liked to walk with her, which is to say, enjoyed her company. Her company, what is it to be in her company?

Once Bebe fell asleep while she was talking to her. Bebe shut her eyes just as she was telling her how eclipsed she felt by everyone. *Am I so dull, so repetitious, so petty?* she was asking this when Bebe's eyes, she saw, were shut.

"You're angry," Bebe said tonight and has said before, along with *You can be mean, you can be judgmental.* Early in the evening Bebe had told her to *stop! Stop complaining!* She had arrived angry and shopped out and sure she had bought the wrong tie and a shirt her husband would never wear but that was because he was so . . . *Stop! You wonder why friends don't want to see you?*

Oh, lady from the suburbs, after too much wine in the city, don't cry!

On the phone again, she clicks off when she hears herself saying . . . "No one is at home . . ."

Not true! Donny might be plugged in somewhere in the house.

And his father, Big D, most likely asleep on the couch, an open book across his chest, a fat hardback on some crisis the usual bullies brought about and then made money fixing.

Big D has very large hands. His hands are so big, he could pulverize the plaster statue of Saint Francis with one of them. She puts her head through the harness of her satchel and moves to take up the luxe bags, but puts them aside again and sits back on the bench.

When Big D was a boy – nine or ten? – he threw potatoes at his mother. While his older brother cheered him on, he pelted her in the back.

Why didn't you stop me, Mother?

Oh, you were only trying to make your brother laugh.

Jokes at the expense of someone else can make Big D laugh, too.

In the picture of this scene, her mother-in-law stands stoutly at the sink dressed in rough linen. The woman's hair is still brown and matches the brown of the sack she wears as a dress. She might be a potato!

Oh, the statue of Saint Francis is pitiably featureless, and she scolds herself for self-pity. Stand up! Quit blubbering! Raise your arms! You're alive! You're well! Think of the war-ravaged poor rocking in a boat in the middle of a black sea, desperate: you're not one of those.

How dark and separate is the house next to the church behind its spiky hedge of arborvitae – who lives there?

She has not always lived in Connecticut.

Once, she knew the lucky girl's life in Maryland. The fields and fences, mown meadow, stubble and stalk, she would like to be back on the footpath to the house on the hill in a rural route setting, a gentleman's farm with a barn and horses cared for by loving staff. Jessup – she misses him. Once gardens simply happened and she, slender, was photographed in them.

House light through the trees but steadily darker along what turns into the stony ledge of road beside genuinely old stone walls where once she used to walk with Lucy, sweet dog.

Why haven't they turned the ledge into a broader path for dog owners – or runners, for that matter, walkers? There are no walkers, that's why – or very few. She might right this imbalance. She might take up walking to the station on the days, like today, when she works in the city.

She steps into the ditch before a car passes but its lights catch parts of her.

She is impossible to miss with these impressive bags and the color of her coat. But her bags! She put them down. She put them down on the bench at Saint Francis Church and never took them up again but walked past them when she left the churchyard. She must not have cared – she doesn't care. Expensive clothes for Big D's big birthday. Sixty.

Is this gift to be returned, I wonder? Is this one for UPS? Big D is well-known to ask of all her gifts as he unwraps them – actually asks of gifts given him by anyone. Big D does not reserve his scorn for her alone.

One for the truck; back on the truck; a doozy for the truck, I'm afraid; load her up; a return, yes, sir, a return – all Big D terms pelted like potatoes, meant to be funny, wasn't, was never oh . . . don't get lost in never-never land.

Once upon a time Big D was *Don* to her and never wrong.

Once upon a time . . . she bought him a green cashmere sweater (he looks good in green) but this green didn't work, and he returned the sweater and came home horrified at how much she had spent on him – but also seeming happy about it. A few weeks later he bought the same sweater on sale in wheat.

She prays her bags fall into needy hands. Do your best, Saint Francis. Besides talking to animals, what else did Saint Francis do? Why is he a saint in the first place? What part of us can he protect?

What a shitty spiritual education she has had, she's simply brushed past churches all of her life, knows a crèche when she sees one.

Across the road and ahead, the pillowy landscape of the golf course and the secular life in light: the River Club badged in deep blue, gold, and white. She owns a lot of RC highball glasses because the River Club is a *big* part of Big D's life. She can turn anything into a joke with *big* at the front.

At this hour the road is not much traveled; its residents, living far apart and withdrawn into their woods and behind their fences, are abed.

Cars pass, several in a row, from a party, perhaps, following each other home – sober drivers, she hopes, soberer than she, yet she moves back in the ditch, which isn't a ditch so much as a broad rut filled with fallen leaves and broken branches, fieldstone and mist rising over a landscape pieced as quaintly as a quilt, and the lady from Connecticut, a loose stitch in it.

ACKNOWLEDGMENTS

Thank you to Diane Williams, great writer, friend, and editor of *NOON*, a literary annual in which most of these stories first appeared. Thank you to Wyatt Prunty for inviting me to his inspiring summer camp, the Sewanee Writers' Conference, where many of these stories first were read. Thank you to Elisabeth Schmitz for her constancy and belief in these stories. Her editorial attentions, along with editor Katie Raissian's notes, greatly improved the collection. A writer's thrill: to be read closely and understood, thank you both for giving the book unity. Thank you to my agent, Gail Hochman, for persevering on my behalf despite hardly Hollywood returns, and to Abby Weintraub, great friend, thank you for another book jacket touched with mystery.

Thank you to my sons, Nicholas and Will Schutt, and to their wives, Bethany LaVoo Schutt and Tania Biancalani, for the ease of mind given a parent when she knows her children are happy. Stay happy. To Maya and Imogen, the grandest of granddaughters, you make me dotty, thank you very much. And for love, and most everything else expressive of it, thank you to my remarkable husband, David Kersey, master gardener and master teacher, the saint who makes this writing life possible. How does it feel to be adored?

Dear readers,

As well as relying on bookshop sales, And Other Stories relies on subscriptions from people like you for many of our books, whose stories other publishers often consider too risky to take on.

Our subscribers don't just make the books physically happen. They also help us approach booksellers, because we can demonstrate that our books already have readers and fans. And they give us the security to publish in line with our values, which are collaborative, imaginative and 'shamelessly literary'.

All of our subscribers:

- receive a first-edition copy of each of the books they subscribe to
- are thanked by name at the end of our subscriber-supported books
- receive little extras from us by way of thank you, for example: postcards created by our authors

BECOME A SUBSCRIBER, OR GIVE A SUBSCRIPTION TO A FRIEND

Visit andotherstories.org/subscribe to help make our books happen. You can subscribe to books we're in the process of making. To purchase books we have already published, we urge you to support your local or favourite bookshop and order directly from them – the often unsung heroes of publishing.

OTHER WAYS TO GET INVOLVED

If you'd like to know about upcoming events and reading groups (our foreign-language reading groups help us choose books to publish, for example) you can:

- join the mailing list at: andotherstories.org/join-us
- follow us on Twitter: @andothertweets
- join us on Facebook: facebook.com/AndOtherStoriesBooks
- admire our books on Instagram: @andotherpics
- follow our blog: andotherstoriespublishing.tumblr.com

This book was made possible thanks to the support of:

Aaron McEnery · Aaron Peck · Aaron Schneider · Abigail Charlesworth · Ada Gokay · Adam Bowman · Adam Butler · Adam Lenson · Agata Rucinska · Ailsa Peate · Aisling Reina · Ajay Sharma · Alan McMonagle · Alan Reid · Alana Marquis-Farncombe · Alastair Gillespie · Alastair Laing · Alex Fleming · Alex Hancock · Alex Liebman · Alex Ramsey · Alexander Bunin · Alexandra Citron · Alexandra de Verseg-Roesch · Alexia Richardson · Alfred Birnbaum · Ali Conway · Ali MacKenzie · Ali Smith · Alice Nightingale · Alice Ramsey · Alison Layland · Alison Lock · Alison MacConnell · Alison Winston · Amanda · Amelia Ashton · Amelia Dowe · Amine Hamadache · Amitav Hajra · Amy Arnold · Amy Benson · Andrea Reece · Andrew Lees · Andrew Marston · Andrew McCallum · Andrew Rego · Andrew Wilkinson · Aneesa Higgins · Angela Everitt · Angus Walker · Anna Glendenning · Anna McKee-Poore · Anna Milsom · Anna Pigott · Anne Carus · Anne Guest · Anne Ryden · Anne Sanders · Anneliese O'Malley · Annie McDermott · Anonymous · Anonymous · Anonymous · Anonymous · Anthony Brown · Anthony Quinn · Antonia Lloyd-Jones · Antonia Saske · Antonio de Swift · Antony Pearce · Aoife Boyd · Archie Davies · Arne Van Petegem · Asako Serizawa · Asher Norris · Audrey Mash · Avril Marren · Ayca Turkoglu · Barbara Mellor · Barbara Wheatley · Barry John Fletcher · Bella Besong · Ben Schofield · Ben Thornton · Benjamin Judge · Beth O'Neill · Bettina Rogerson · Beverly Jackson · Bianca Jackson · Bianca Winter · Björn Halldórsson · Blythe Ridge Sloan · Brandon Knibbs · Brendan McIntyre · Briallen Hopper · Brian Byrne · Bridget Gill · Bridget Starling · Brigid O'Connor · Brigita Ptackova · Caitlin Halpern · Caitlin Liebenberg · Callie Steven · Cameron Lindo · Caren Harple · Carla Carpenter · Carol Christie · Carol-Ann Davids & Micah Naidoo · Carol Laurent · Carolina Pineiro · Caroline Bennett · Caroline Lodge · Caroline Picard · Caroline Smith · Caroline Waight · Caroline West · Carolyn Johnson · Cassidy Hughes · Catherine Lambert · Catherine Taylor · Catriona Gibbs · Cecilia Rossi · Cecilia Uribe · Cecily Maude · Chantal Wright · Charles Fernyhough · Charles Dee Mitchell · Charles Raby · Charles Wolfe · Charlotte Briggs · Charlotte Holtam · Charlotte Murrie & Stephen Charles · Charlotte Ryland · Charlotte Whittle · Chia Foon Yeow · China Miéville · Chris Gribble · Chris Holmes · Chris Hughes · Chris Nielsen · Chris & Kathleen Repper-Day · Chris Stevenson · Chris Young · Christina Harris · Christine Bartels · Christine Dyer · Christine Hudnall · Christine Luker · Christopher Allen · Christopher Stout · Christopher Terry · Ciara Ní Riain · Claire Adams · Claire Ashman · Claire Malcolm · Claire Tristram · Claire Williams · Clare Archibald · Clarice Borges · Claudia Hoare · Claudia Nannini · Clifford Posner · Clive Bellingham · Clive Hewat · Cody Copeland · Colin Matthews · Colin Prendergast · Corey Nelson · Cornelia van der Weide · Courtney Lilly · Craig Barney · Dan Parkinson · Daniel Arnold · Daniel Coxon · Daniel Douglas · Daniel Gallimore · Daniel Gillespie · Daniel Hahn · Daniel Kennedy · Daniel Manning · Daniel Reid · Daniel Sparling · Daniel Sweeney · Daniel Syrovy · Daniel Venn · Daniela Steierberg · Darcy Hurford · Dave Lander · Dave Young · Davi Rocha · David Anderson · David Hebblethwaite · David Higgins · David Johnson-Davies · David F Long · David Mantero · David Miller · David Shriver · David Smith · David Steege · David Travis · Dean Taucher · Debbie Pinfold · Declan O'Driscoll · Deirdre Nic

Mhathuna · Delaina Haslam · Denis Larose · Dominick Santa Cattarina · Dominique Brocard · Donald Wilson · Duncan Clubb · Duncan Marks · Ed Owles · Edward Rathke · Ekaterina Beliakova · Elaine Rassaby · Eleanor Dawson · Eleanor Maier · Elhum Shakerifar · Elie Howe · Elina Zicmane · Elisabeth Cook · Eliza Apperly · Eliza O'Toole · Elizabeth Draper · Elizabeth Farnsworth · Ellen Coopersmith · Ellen Kennedy · Ellen Wilkinson · Ellie Goddard · Emily Bromfield · Emily Chia & Marc Ronnie · Emily Howe · Emily Taylor · Emily Williams · Emily Yaewon Lee & Gregory Limpens · Emma Barraclough · Emma Bielecki · Emma Louise Grove · Emma Perry · Emma Reynolds · Emma Strong · Emma Teale · Emma Timpany · Emma Turesson · Emma Yearwood · Erin Braybrook · Erin Cameron Allen · Erin Louttit · Ewan Tant · F Gary Knapp · Fatima Kried · Fawzia Kane · Filiz Emre-Cooke · Finbarr Farragher · Fiona Malby · Fiona Mozley · Fiona Quinn · Florence Reynolds · Florian Duijsens · Fran Sanderson · Francesca Brooks · Francisco Vilhena · Frank van Orsouw · Friederike Knabe · Gabriela Lucia Garza de Linde · Gabrielle Crockatt · Gary Gorton · Gavin Collins · Gavin Smith · Gawain Espley · Genaro Palomo Jr · Geoff Copps · Geoff Fisher · Geoff Thrower · Geoffrey Cohen · Geoffrey Urland · George Christie · George Hawthorne · George McCaig · George Stanbury · George Wilkinson · Georgia Panteli · Geraldine Brodie · Gill Boag-Munroe · Gillian Ackroyd · Gillian Bohnet · Gillian Grant · Glen Bornais · Gordon Cameron · Graham R Foster · Grant Hartwell · Grant Rintoul · Gregory Ford · Guy Haslam · Gwyn Lewis · Hadil Balzan · Hank Pryor · Hannah Mayblin · Hannah Richter · Hannah Stevens · Hannah Stogdon · Hans Krensler · Hans Lazda · Harmony Chan · Hattie Edmonds · Heather Tipon · Heidi James · Helen Asquith · Helen Bailey · Helen Bowell · Helen Brady · Helen Collins · Helen Gough · Helen & Michael Pope · Helen White · Helen Wormald · Henrike Laehnemann · Henry Patino · HL Turner-Heffer · Holly Pester · Howard Robinson · Hugh Gilmore · Iain Munro · Ian Barnett · Ian Docherty · Ian McMillan · Ián Mond · Ian Randall · Ieva Panavaite & Mariusz Hubski · Ingrid Olsen · Irene Mansfield · Irina Tzanova · Isabella Garment · Isabella Weibrecht · Isobel Dixon · J Collins · Jacinta Perez Gavilan Torres · Jack Brown · Jackie Sullivan · Jacqueline Haskell · Jacqueline Lademann · Jacqueline Ting Lin · Jacqueline Vint · James Attlee · James Beck · James Crossley · James Cubbon · James Lesniak · James Portlock · James Purdon · James Scudamore · James Tierney · Jamie Osborn · Jamie Walsh · Jane Mark-Lawson · Jane Roberts · Jane Williams · Jane Woollard · Janet Kay · Janet Sarbanes · Janette Ryan · Janne Støen · Jasmine Gideon · Jason Shaver · JC Sutcliffe · Jean-Jacques Regouffre · Jeanne Guyon · Jeff Collins · Jenifer Logie · Jennifer Arnold · Jennifer Bernstein · Jennifer Higgins · Jennifer Humbert · Jennifer Petersen · Jenny Booth · Jenny Huth · Jenny Newton · Jeremy Koenig · Jess Howard-Armitage · Jesse Coleman · Jessica Billington · Jessica Kibler · Jessica Loveland · Jethro Soutar · Jill Twist · Jillian Jones · Jim Boucherat · Jo Goodall · Jo Harding · Jo Lateu · Joan O'Malley · Joanna Flower · Joanna Luloff · Joao Pedro Bragatti Winckler · JoDee Brandon · Jodie Adams · Johan Forsell · Johan Trouw · Johanna Anderson · Johanna Eliasson · Johannes Georg Zipp · John Berube · John Conway · John Coyne · John Down · John Gent · John Hodgson · John Kelly · John McGill · John McKee · John Royley · John Shaw · John Steigerwald · John Winkelman · Jon Riches · Jonathan Blaney · Jonathan Huston · Jonathan Kiehlmann · Jonathan Watkiss · Jorge Cino · Joseph Cooney · Joseph Schreiber · Joshua Davis · Judith Martens · Julia Hays · Julia Rochester · Julia

Sutton-Mattocks · Julian Duplain · Julian Lomas · Julie Gibson · Julie Gibson · Juliet Swann · Julius Roberts · JW Mersky · Kaarina Hollo · Kapka Kassabova · Kara Kogler Baptista · Karen Faarbaek de Andrade Lima · Karen Jones · Karen Waloschek · Kasim Husain · Kasper Haakansson · Kasper Hartmann · Kate Attwooll · Kate Gardner · Kate Griffin · Kate McLarnon · Katharina Liehr · Katharine Freeman · Katharine Nurse · Katharine Robbins · Katherine El-Salahi · Katherine Mackinnon · Katherine Skala · Katherine Sotejeff-Wilson · Kathryn Cave · Kathryn Edwards · Kathryn Kasimor · Kathryn Williams · Katie Brown · Katrina Thomas · Keith Walker · Kenneth Blythe · Kent McKernan · Kevin Porter · Khairunnisa Ibrahim · Kieron James · Kim Gormley · Kirsten Major · Kirsty Doole · KL Ee · Kristin Djuve · Kristina Rudinskas · Lana Selby · Larraine Gooch · Laura Batatota · Laura Brown · Laura Lea · Lauren Ellemore · Lauren Hyett · Lauren Rea · Laurence Laluyaux · Laurie Sheck & Jim Peck · Leah Cooper · Leah Good · Leon Frey · Leonie Schwab · Leonie Smith · Leri Price · Lesley Lawn · Lesley Watters · Leslie Wines · Liam Buell · Liam Elward · Liliana Lobato · Lily Levinson · Lindsay Brammer · Lindsey Stuart · Lindy van Rooyen · Lisa Taylor · Liz Ketch · Liz Wilding · Lizzie Broadbent ·

Loretta Platts · Lori Frecker · Lorna Bleach · Lorna Scott Fox · Lorraine Bachand · Lorraine Bramwell · Lottie Smith · Louise Musson · Louise Piper · Louise Thompson · Luc Daley · Luc Verstraete · Lucia Rotheray · Lucy Goy · Lucy Hariades · Lucy Moffatt · Lucy Summers · Lucy Wheeler · Luke Healey · Luke Williamson · Lynn Martin · M Manfre · Madeleine Kleinwort · Maeve Lambe · Maggie Livesey · Mahan L Ellison & K Ashley Dickson · Mairi Contos · Mandy Wight · Marcia Walker · Margaret Jull Costa · Maria Hill · Marie Cloutier · Marie Donnelly · Marina Castledine · Mario Cianci · Mario Sifuentez · Marja S Laaksonen · Mark Langston · Mark Sargent · Mark & Sarah Sheets · Mark Sztyber · Mark Waters · Marlene Adkins · Martha Nicholson · Martin Munro · Martin Price · Martin Vosyka · Martin Whelton · Mary Byrne · Mary Carozza · Mary Ellen Nagle · Mary Wang · Marzieh Youssefi · Matt Klein · Matt & Owen Davies · Matt Sosnow · Matthew Adamson · Matthew Armstrong · Matthew Banash · Matthew Francis · Matthew Hamblin · Matthew Lowe · Matthew McKeever · Matthew Smith · Matthew Thomas · Matthew Warshauer · Matthew Woodman · Matty Ross · Maureen Pritchard · Max Garrone · Max Longman · Maxim Grigoriev · Meaghan

Delahunt · Megan Wittling · Melissa Beck · Melissa da Silveira Serpa · Melissa Danny · Melissa Quignon-Finch · Meredith Jones · Merima Jahic · Mette Kongsted · Michael Aguilar · Michael Andal · Michael Bichko · Michael Coutts · Michael Gavin · Michael James Eastwood · Michael Moran · Michael Ward · Michelle Falkoff · Michelle Lotherington · Michelle Roberts · Mike Bittner · Mike Timms · Mike Turner · Milo Waterfield · Miriam McBride · Mitchell Albert · Molly Foster · Monica Anderson · Monika Olsen · Morgan Lyons · MP Boardman · Myles Nolan · N Tsolak · Namita Chakrabarty · Nancy Foley · Nancy Oakes · Naomi Kruger · Natalie Smith · Natasha Wightman · Nathalie Atkinson · Nathan Dorr · Navi Sahota · Neil George · Neil Pretty · Nicholas Brown · Nick Chapman · Nick Flegel · Nick James · Nick Nelson & Rachel Eley · Nick Rombes · Nick Sidwell · Nick Twemlow · Nicola Hart · Nicola Mira · Nicola Sandiford · Nicole Matteini · Nicoletta Asciuto · Nikki Brice · Nikolaj Ramsdal Nielsen · Nina Alexandersen · Nina de la Mer · Nina Moore · Nina Power · Noah Levin · Olga Brawanska · Olga Zilberbourg · Oliver Keens · Olivia Payne · Olivia Tweed · P Mackarness · Pamela Ritchie · Pashmina Murthy · Pat Bevins · Patricia Appleyard · Patrick William · Paul

Cray · Paul Daw · Paul Griffiths · Paul Jones · Paul Munday · Paul Myatt · Paul Robinson · Paul Segal · Paula Edwards · Paula Ely · Penelope Hewett Brown · Penny East · Pete Stephens · Peter McBain · Peter McCambridge · Peter Rowland · Peter Vos · Peter Wells · Philip Carter · Philip Nulty · Philip Warren · Philipp Jarke · Phillip Featherstone · Piet Van Bockstal · PM Goodman · Polly Walshe · Portia Msimang · PRAH Foundation · Rachael Williams · Rachel Andrews · Rachel Barnes · Rachel Carter · Rachel Lasserson · Rachel Matheson · Rachel Van Riel · Rachel Wadham · Rachel Watkins · Rachel Wysoker · Rachele Huennekens · Raeanne Lambert · Ralph Cowling · Rebecca Braun · Rebecca Carter · Rebecca Fearnley · Rebecca Moss · Rebecca Rosenthal · Rebekah Hughes · Rhiannon Armstrong · Richard Ashcroft · Richard Bauer · Richard Mansell · Richard McClelland · Richard Priest · Richard Shea · Richard Soundy · Rishi Dastidar · Robert Gillett · Robert Hugh-Jones · Roberta Allport · Robin Taylor · Roger Newton · Rory Williamson · Rosalind Ramsay · Rose Crichton · Rosemary Rodwell · Rosie Pinhorn · Rowena McWilliams · Roxanne O'Del Ablett · Roz Simpson · Rozzi Hufton · Rupert Ziziros · Sabine Griffiths · Sabrina Uswak · Sally Baker · Sally Dowell · Sally Foreman · Sally Thomson · Sam Gordon · Sam Reese · Sam Ruddock · Sam Stern · Samantha Murphy · Samantha Sawers · Samantha Smith · Samantha Walton · Samuel Daly · Sandra Mayer · Sara Di Girolamo · Sarah Arboleda · Sarah Harwood · Sarah Jacobs · Sarah Lucas · Sarah Pybus · Sarah Watkins · Sarah Wollner · Satara Lazar · Scott Thorough · Sean Birnie · Sean Kelly · Sean Malone · Sean McGivern · Sejal Shah · SH Makdisi · Shannon Beckner · Shannon Knapp · Shauna Gilligan · Sheridan Marshall · Sherman Alexie · Shira Lob · Shirley Harwood · Sian Rowe · Sigurjon Sigurdsson · Simon Armstrong · Simon James · Simon Pitney · Simon Robertson · Simone O'Donovan · Sindre Bjugn · Siriol Hugh-Jones · SJ Bradley · SK Grout · Sofia Mostaghimi · Sonia McLintock · Sonia Pelletreau · Sophia Wickham · Srikanth Reddy · ST Dabbagh · Stacy Rodgers · Stefanie May IV · Stefano Mula · Stephan Eggum · Stephanie Lacava · Stephen Pearsall · Stu Sherman · Stuart Wilkinson · Subhasree Basu · Sue & Ed Aldred · Susan Higson · Susan Irvine · Susan Manser · Susanna Fidoe · Susie Roberson · Suzanne Lee · Sylvie Zannier-Betts · Tamara Larsen · Tammy Watchorn · Tania Hershman · Tanja Heller · Ted Burness · Teresa Griffiths · Teresa Werner · Terry Kurgan · Tessa Lang · The Rookery In the Bookery · Thomas Baker · Thomas Bell · Thomas Fritz · Thomas Legendre · Thomas Mitchell · Thomas O'Rourke · Thomas Rowley · Thomas van den Bout · Tiffany Lehr · Tim Hopkins · Tim & Pavlina Morgan · Tim Theroux · Timothy Owen · Tina Andrews · Tina Rotherham-Winqvist · TJ Clark · Todd Greenwood · Tom Atkins · Tom Darby · Tom Dixon · Tom Franklin · Tom Gray · Tom Stafford · Tom Whatmore · Tom Wilbey · Tony Bastow · Tony Messenger · Torna Russell-Hills · Tory Jeffay · Tracy Northup · Tracy Shapley · Tracy Washington · Trevor Lewis · Trevor Wald · Val Challen · Valerie Hamra · Vanessa Nolan · Vanessa Rush · Veronica Barnsley · Victor Meadowcroft · Victoria Adams · Victoria Maitland · Victoria Smith · Vijay Pattisapu · Vikki O'Neill · Vilis Kasims · Vinod Vijayakumar · Virginia Weir · Visaly Muthusamy · Wendy Langridge · Wendy Peate · Will Huxter · William Brockenborough · William Dennehy · William Mackenzie · Yoora Yi Tenen · Zoë Brasier

Current & Upcoming Books

CHRISTINE SCHUTT is the author of two short story collections and three novels. She has been a finalist for both the National Book Award (Florida) and Pulitzer Prize (All Souls). Among other honours, Schutt has twice won the O. Henry Award for her stories. She is the recipient of the New York Foundation of the Arts and Guggenheim Fellowships. Schutt lives and teaches in New York.